The Awesome Bird

"This is the first Really Unexpected Thing that's ever happened to me," said Laurie. "You're more than Out-of-the-Blue, you're the first proper adventure that's come my way. Do we have far to go? Are we going to the Island? Are we going There? And who is the Rabobab?"

The Bird didn't answer of course. Its wings had found a smooth and regular rhythm that gradually soothed Laurie into silence. He let his head sink into the soft warm feathers of the Bird's neck and then he slept.

In his sleep he thought he heard the Bird singing and the song somehow reminded him of Ginger's fiddle, only it was a sweeter, slower tune and although it had no words, Laurie knew it was the Song of the Island.

DIANA HENDRY BOOKS IN RED FOX

Harvey Angell
The Awesome Bird

The Awesome Bird

DIANA HENDRY

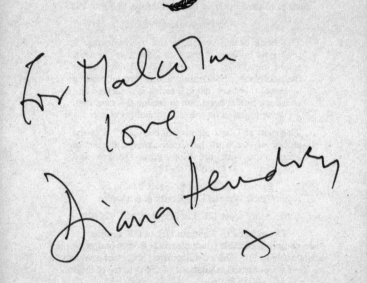

For Malcolm
love,

Diana Hendry
x

RED FOX

A Red Fox Book

Published by Random House Children's Books
20 Vauxhall Bridge Road, London SW1V 2SA

A division of Random House UK Ltd
London Melbourne Sydney Auckland
Johannesburg and agencies throughout the world

Copyright © Diana Hendry 1995

1 3 5 7 9 10 8 6 4 2

First published in Great Britain by Julia MacRae 1995

Red Fox edition 1997

Printed and bound in Great Britain by
Cox & Wyman Ltd, Reading, Berkshire

Random House UK Limited Reg. No. 954009

Papers used by Random House UK Limited
are natural, recyclable products made from wood grown in
sustainable forests. The manufacturing processes conform to
the environmental regulations of the country of origin.

ISBN 0 09 960521 X

CONTENTS

For my sister, Leila – with love

The lines quoted on p. 112 are from 'Four Things to Remember When Writing a Poem' by John Mole, from *Catching a Spider*, Blackie.

Between two worlds life hovers like a star,
    'Twixt night and morn, upon the horizon's verge.
How little do we know that which we are!
    How less what we may be!

Byron

CHAPTER 1

A Haunting

At first Laurie thought the bird was an owl. A white owl. A snowy owl. A decidedly mad owl. An owl badly in need of a pair of spectacles, for night after night it came knocking at Laurie's bedroom window. Its sharp beak rat-tatted at the window as if tapping out some urgent message in Morse. Its large wings batted against the pane as if by much flapping it might flap itself right through the glass.

It was the largest bird Laurie had ever seen, far larger than an owl, in fact, but remembering the bird in the morning, Laurie thought that perhaps the shock of waking, not to darkness, but to the spread of the bird's bright white wings filling his window, had simply made it seem enormous. And then Laurie only knew city birds – sparrows and robins, fierce black rooks that seemed tough enough to survive the city and pigeons grey as the pavements. An owl was the largest bird Laurie could name.

If, at the beginning, Laurie had told someone about these night visits of the bird, then things might have been very different. But then Laurie had doubts. He was prone to vivid dreams and bouts of restlessness which sent him walking for miles without quite knowing why. Both the dreams and the walks – even though he always took Puddles with him – were things that made his mother frowningly anxious, as if there was something dangerous about both dreams and restlessness.

And then although Laurie knew it was real, not a dream bird, it seemed to have that mysterious dream-like quality about it. The very softness of its feathers, its whiteness against the night sky, seemed to say, 'Hush, hush. Tell no-one.' It was private, this bird, like your most secret hopes.

And it was haunting. Laurie's day-time life, which in any case seemed dull and drab, was made even more so by comparison with the bird's arrival – large, beautiful, magical – on the balcony in front of his bedroom. When the bird appeared, balancing on the black iron railing, the whole city, with its night lights and stars, faded out of existence behind the white beauty of its outstretched wings.

It was autumn. "Perhaps," said Laurie to Puddles when they were out on one of their walks, "the bird is the harbinger of snow." (Talking to Puddles didn't count as telling anyone about the bird. Puddles was just the perfect listener.) Laurie liked the word 'harbinger'. He'd heard it in a poem at school, something about the first primrose being the harbinger of spring. But the idea of the bird as a harbinger of snow seemed silly.

"Or perhaps he comes from another world," said Laurie. But even Puddles, who was quite used to hearing the maddest of notions, clearly thought this one very silly. He went bounding ahead of Laurie on his long curly-haired legs, his ears (which were like the triangular flaps of envelopes) flapping and his long tail curling up into a question mark as if to say, 'You can't be serious?'

So Laurie didn't voice what was, perhaps, his silliest thought of all – which was that once upon a time he had known something about this other world and that the coming of the bird had something to do with Ginger.

But it was this, the silliest thought, that nagged at Laurie. And so when the bird had appeared on the balcony for three nights on the run – or on the wing – Laurie suddenly felt that the question mark of Puddles' tail wasn't quite enough by way of human response. It was high time, sky-high, bird-in-the-night time, to talk to Ginger.

CHAPTER 2

Something Out of the Blue

Ginger lived in a van at the bottom of Laurie's road. Umberton Road was on the edge of the city. Rather it was where the city ran out and the country didn't quite begin – a sort of nowhere place.

The road itself wasn't even a proper road. It didn't go anywhere. It was set high above a railway track and ran down to a narrow lane where dozens of allotments began. There was a bridge over the railway track, and long streets of houses, going every which way as if over on *that* side of the bridge, everything was homely. But on Laurie's side, on the Umberton Road side, there was just Clampitt Court, three square blocks of flats sticking out of the hillside like three huge teeth in a raw gum.

The flats looked as if they'd been stuck up there out of everyone's way or because nothing else would grow there. And nothing much did. There was some scruffy grass between the blocks that was too trampled on and too shadowed to grow properly, and at the back there was a line of wilting sycamores. The trees looked as if they had considered the height of the flats, said to themselves, 'We'll never grow *that* high,' and given up.

Strictly speaking, dogs were not allowed in the flats.

But Puddles had been a stray, a shivering puppy found one winter by Laurie and his mother, Mrs O'Grady, lapping water out of a puddle.

They had taken him to the police station and when, after seven days, no-one had claimed him, Mrs O'Grady looked at Laurie and Laurie looked at his mother and without a word they put on their coats and went to collect him. And Puddles was such a cheerful, welcoming sort of dog and the question mark of his tail seemed so clearly to be saying, 'You do like me, don't you?' that none of the residents of Clampitt Court could resist him. Puddles stayed.

All the flats had balconies and things *did* grow there. Pots of geraniums and trailing ivies. Lines of washing. Toys. Grannies in old chairs. Gossiping mothers.

It was one Sunday afternoon in April that from his balcony – the balcony of Flat 6, Block B – Laurie saw Ginger arrive. He came in such a rattly, funny-looking daffodil yellow van that it made Laurie laugh out loud.

Sunday afternoon was the dullest time of all in Umberton Road. Anyone who was going to wash a car, walk a dog, or water a geranium had already done it. Late on Sunday afternoon the residents of Clampitt Court sank into a torpor before their videos and televisions and waited for next week to begin.

Laurie had taken Puddles for a rainy walk in the park. Now Puddles lay stretched out before one bar of the electric fire, drying and giving off a damp, doggy smell, much like old socks.

As usual on a Sunday afternoon, Mrs O'Grady was absorbed in a magazine competition. Mrs O'Grady did a lot of competitions, though she rarely won anything. Two red mugs, a tin opener that didn't work properly, a set of wine glasses they never used and an awful china cherub had been her prizes so far.

But Mrs O'Grady liked making up the rhymes and slogans for the competitions.

"What's this one for?" asked Laurie.

"A car," said Mrs O'Grady.

"You can't drive," said Laurie.

His mother ignored this. "I need a rhyme," she said. "Two lines on why the Mini Moffat is the best car on the market."

Laurie was well practised in making up rhymes.

> "The Mini Moffat's small and snappy,
> Keeps you snug as a baby's nappy,"

he suggested.

"I don't think that will do," said Mrs O'Grady. "Anyway, I could learn to drive, Laurie B. Mrs Naylor said she'd teach me."

(Laurie's mother often called him Laurie B. Partly because his second name was Benedict, but more because she said Laurie was a name that floated off in the air at the end and needed bringing down to earth again, which was what the 'B' did for it.)

"Mrs Naylor's had three prangs already this year," said Laurie.

"The best teachers are those who know the difficulties of the thing they are teaching," said Mrs O'Grady loftily. "And now I need to concentrate."

Puddles turned over to steam his other side. Laurie sighed and went along to his bedroom and out on to the balcony just in case anything – anything that might look even remotely exciting – was going on in Umberton Road.

And then he saw it. At least first he heard it. A rattling,

rasping, spluttering noise and then there it was – a bright yellow van decorated with what looked like swirly-legged blue octopuses and sporting a little tin chimney pot, striped, like a barber's pole.

The engine's death-rattle carried on for fully two minutes after the van had stopped, then it shuddered into silence as if it was wholly exhausted and out got a very small and skinny woman wearing innumerable skirts and cardigans. And after her came an equally skinny boy with tufty ginger hair and a lot of freckles.

The trio – van, woman and boy – were the cheeriest thing Laurie had ever seen in Umberton Road. His heart leapt at the sight of them. They had about them something that Laurie hungered and hankered for but found difficult to name; something he glimpsed in his vivid dreams; something he almost touched and tasted when he kicked his way through autumn leaves or saw the trees in the park burst into spring life.

It was, he thought, gazing at the brightness of the van, the skirts of many colours worn by the woman, the ginger of Ginger's hair which reminded Laurie of fireworks on bonfire night, something to do with colour. Colour and excitement. It was as if these two lived life by a different set of rules – rules that made you feel more alive instead of less alive. They looked, thought Laurie, as if they lived Bright-Yellow-and-Ginger lives.

And Laurie's own life in Umberton Road felt grey. It was all right in its way, of course, but it was a dull way. A regular way. A Scouts-on-Tuesday, violin-lesson-on-Thursday, supermarket-shopping-on-Friday and silly-competition-rhymes-on-Sunday way. Walking Puddles was fun, of course. But not *that* much fun on your own. And the worst thing of all was that Laurie couldn't see any of this changing. It would just go on like this, greyly, for what felt like forever and ever amen, when what he wanted was something Unexpected. Something Out of the Blue. (Or perhaps it should be Out of the Grey.) Something that made you say, "Well, I'd never have guessed!"

Laurie watched the woman standing on the embankment above the railway track, hands on her hips, looking about her – at the allotments running down the lane, at the bridge over the track and the tiers of houses beyond it, at the gaunt blocks of flats.

She seemed to think Umberton Road would do, for she nodded at the boy and he went back into the van and brought out a camping stove. Very soon they began frying sausages.

Laurie ran along to his mother.

"Come and look out here," he said.

Mrs O'Grady came to the window carrying her magazine and chewing her pencil. But she dropped both when she saw the bright yellow van and the woman and boy frying sausages.

"Susan!" said Mrs O'Grady. "Susan Smiley!"

But she said it as if she was really saying, 'Doom!'

CHAPTER 3

Sort of Ginger

"You know her?" asked Laurie. He felt very impressed. Laurie heard of other mothers who knew interesting people. Other mothers knew people who had appeared on television or had brothers in Australia or uncles who were astronomers or astronauts, but until now Laurie's own mother hadn't come up with any friend or relative of greater interest than a stamp-collecting cousin in Somerset and accident-prone Mrs Naylor.

"Do I know Susan?" replied Mrs O'Grady as if Laurie had asked her if she knew her own name and address.

But as for *how* she knew Susan, or *when* she knew Susan or *where* or *why*, Mrs O'Grady simply wouldn't tell, not then, not until much, much later.

"It's all so long ago, I couldn't begin," she said. "And don't start nagging me, Laurie B. There are some things you are better off *not* knowing. And if I were you, I wouldn't start making friends with that boy because he'll be gone before you know it."

And of course the moment she said this Laurie decided – decided there and then on that very first Sunday afternoon – that that was just what he *did* want to do, make friends with Ginger.

9

Laurie couldn't work out what his mother thought of their strange new neighbours. She wasn't pleased by their arrival, that much was certain. But somehow or other she seemed keen to look after them. She took them things. Soup. A pot of jam. A cardigan she no longer wore for Susan or some jerseys Laurie had grown out of for Ginger.

Sometimes, when he came home from school, Laurie found Susan and his mother sharing a cup of tea outside the van – Mrs O'Grady always refused to go inside the van – and there was a look about them as if they had been talking about something really interesting but had stopped as soon as Laurie appeared. And then his mother always hurried him home insisting it was teatime or Scouts time or violin practice time.

It wasn't easy making friends with Ginger.

Ginger was a loner. Often, on his way to school, Laurie saw him pushing an old go-cart (made out of a wooden box and a set of old pram wheels) over the bridge. And at lunch time Laurie had seen him coming back with the go-cart full of old books.

Mostly Ginger looked puzzled. Seriously puzzled: his thin, freckled face screwed up as if there were hundreds of questions in his head and his ginger hair sticking up in a permanently startled, surprised-to-be-here sort of way.

Unlike Susan, who wore layers and layers of clothes, Ginger always wore the same thing – jeans and a vest. The vest revealed a small bright bluebird tattooed on the top of his arm.

And he always looked busy. As if he had a job of work to do. And this was odd because he didn't go to school, he had lessons with Susan in the van.

"Probably old folk lore and magic arts," said Mrs O'Grady darkly while making a very plain cottage pie.

Secretly, Laurie hoped his mother was right. He felt sure that Susan had far more interesting things to teach than his own teachers at Crickleston Junior.

But although Ginger waved when he saw Laurie, and although Susan smiled in a way that made you think 'smiley' was just the right second name for her, there was no chat, no conversation. And Laurie's eagerness to make friends made him so shy that he didn't know how to begin.

It was Puddles who did it of course.

Out walking with Puddles one Sunday morning, they saw Ginger sitting on the embankment above the railway track and without more ado Puddles rushed up to Ginger, wagging his question mark and giving Ginger a thorough licking. And Ginger fell over backwards laughing. Then Laurie laughed too and sat down on the bank beside Ginger, and that was it, they were friends.

But it was an odd, uneasy kind of friendship. There were things you could ask Ginger and things you couldn't.

For instance, one day when they were out book-collecting with the go-cart, Laurie asked, "Is Susan your mother?"

"Sort of," said Ginger.

"Or your aunt?" persisted Laurie.

"Sort of," said Ginger again.

"Or your sister?" demanded Laurie.

"Sort of," said Ginger.

"Well, she can't possibly be 'sort of' all three!" cried Laurie, thoroughly exasperated, for after all it was bad enough his mother refusing – as she still refused – to tell him how she came to know Susan without all these 'sort ofs'.

"Must go," said Ginger, and disappeared down a side

street leaving Laurie and Puddles alone and surprised outside a bookshop which had boxes and boxes of books out on the pavement all marked at 10p or 20p.

But the next time they met, Ginger would be as friendly as ever. "Let's walk down to the allotments," he'd say. Or, "Let's explore the flats."

Exploring the flats was one of Ginger's interests that Laurie found hard to understand. Ginger liked to go up and down the four flights of stairs and look at the different coloured doors and hear the different noises coming from inside – the sound of a piano, radio or television; people talking or laughing or shouting. Ginger liked to hear about the Bennetts (second floor, blue door) where there was always the murmur of earnest conversation, or Mr Kittoe (top floor, yellow door) where there was much piano practicing, or the Hamilton twins ('double trouble', Mrs O'Grady called them) who lived on the ground floor (green door) and were always fighting.

In fact one way and another, there was little Ginger *didn't* want to know about. Laurie noticed that the books Ginger most liked to collect were old encyclopaedias, history books, books about birds and animals, poetry books. And whenever they were out walking Puddles together – which all through summer they did a lot – Ginger liked to know the names of things. Of people, trees, birds, buildings.

It was as if, Laurie thought to himself from time to time, Ginger was doing research of some kind. But what kind? And for who?

And there was another odd thing. Sometimes Ginger would say, "Susan's calling me." And they were miles and miles from home. When they did get back to the van it was usually to find Susan singing and dancing.

"I do believe she *sings* him home," Laurie said to Puddles and Puddles yawned as if to say, "Yes, of course. What could be more natural?"

Mrs O'Grady kept up her line in Dark Warnings about Ginger Going Off at any moment, but she gave up trying to keep the boys apart and Laurie became a regular visitor to the van.

The van itself was not unlike a travelling library. There were shelves of books all along one side of it. The space under the two bunk beds was packed with books and the table, at which Susan and Ginger sat at lesson time, was a long plank of wood resting on a base of books.

The lessons themselves were rather disappointing and not nearly as exciting as Mrs O'Grady imagined them to be. They seemed to involve Ginger in giving a long and detailed description of everything he had seen and heard that day. Susan seemed to want to know all the sights, sounds, smells – even the taste and touch of things. And then Ginger made long lists of everything in a small fat red notebook.

Sometimes, when Ginger forgot something he had seen, Laurie would fill in for him. "You've forgotten to mention that the third allotment has a shed and the fifth one only grows flowers," he would say. Or "You've missed out the library windows – it's got one round one, like a port-hole."

And Susan would say, "Look! Look, Ginger! You must look!"

Perhaps, Laurie thought, all this looking and list-making was just Susan's way of keeping things tidy. Mothers were like that. And if you only had a small van to keep tidy, well, maybe you extended outwards and tried to keep everything about you tidy too. Put the world down in a notebook and it was tucked up tidy as in a drawer or cupboard.

'For later use', a voice whispered in Laurie's head. But he ignored this – or until the coming of the Awesome Bird he ignored it. Mostly Laurie just enjoyed being at home in the van. For at home was how he felt – among the books and the wood-burning stove that Susan kept constantly on the go, whatever the weather, and the two oil lamps that swung gently from hooks in the van's roof.

"Don't think you can *be* Ginger," Mrs O'Grady said crossly when he came home, late again, from a visit to the van. It seemed a strange thing to say. Laurie felt as different from Ginger as anyone could possibly be. Ginger liked facts. Laurie liked dreams. Ginger could play the fiddle as if his fingers found the notes by magic. Laurie could only scrape a slow tune. Yet *with* Ginger, with Ginger and Susan in the van he felt – well, somehow more himself. More Laurie.

One day when Laurie came home from school he found his mother sitting on the floor cutting out a dress from some yellow and purple spotted material.

"Is that for you?" asked Laurie, surprised, for mostly his mother wore pale pinks and blues.

"It's for Susan," said Mrs O'Grady, keeping her head bent over the material and not looking at Laurie.

Laurie flopped on to the sofa and Puddles immediately jumped up beside him and curled into – well, into a puddle.

"If you don't like Susan . . ." began Laurie.

"I never said I didn't *like* her," said his mother, snappy as her scissors.

"All right, then. But you didn't seem exactly pleased when she arrived and you don't like me being friends with

Ginger. So why are you making Susan a dress? Why do you give her presents?"

Mrs O'Grady sighed and put down her scissors.

"A long time ago Susan did me a big favour," she said. "And there are some people who are in your life – a part of your life – whether you want them to be or not. Susan's one of those. Now I don't want any more questions."

But Laurie couldn't stop. "Well, what about Ginger then? Ginger might be just one of those sort of people for me. Someone who's in my life whether *you* like it or not!"

Mrs O'Grady looked at Laurie silently. She looked so suddenly sad that Laurie felt ashamed of himself and went off to do his homework.

Some nights Laurie and his mother watched from the window of the flat as Ginger played his fiddle and Susan danced.

"It gives me the creeps," said Mrs O'Grady when the fiddle started up, usually about ten o'clock, and they could see Susan stamping, stomping and whirling, her layers of skirts and petticoats twirling like a Catherine wheel. "And all the residents are beginning to complain."

"Where did he learn to play like that?" asked Laurie enviously. "Without music." In his own violin lessons Laurie could only manage a very slow and rather squeaky melody.

"He plays by ear," said Mrs O'Grady. "Some people just can. But I can't say I like the tunes he plays – they're . . . they're unearthly!" and Mrs O'Grady shuddered and shut the window.

Laurie wasn't sure he liked the tunes either. They were strange wisps of melodies that seemed to hang about in the evening air like scraps of clouds that had drifted away from some larger cloud. And then the tunes grew faster and faster, turned into gigues that made you feel you might burst if you didn't dance.

"Why don't we go down and join them?" Laurie suggested one night.

"I've told you already, Laurie B," said his mother, "Susan and Ginger live a very different life to ours."

And that's just why I like them, thought Laurie.

Mrs O'Grady looked at Laurie staring moodily out of the window. "Ginger's not an ordinary sort of boy," she said more gently. "It won't pay to get fond of him, Laurie."

Angrily Laurie went off to bed. He could still hear Ginger's fiddle as he lay there and his mother's words echoed in his head. 'Susan and Ginger. They live a very different life to ours. Ginger's not an ordinary boy. It won't pay to get fond of him.'

Fond. That was just the daft sort of word his mother would use. Fond wasn't what Laurie felt. Fascinated was more like it. Fascinated, curious, envious – and yes, mixed in with all that, just plain friendly!

And that's how he continued to feel all summer as he and Ginger explored the city together, pushing the go-cart, being pulled along by Puddles; sitting on the railway embankment naming the wild flowers and the occasional butterfly; talking about the people in the flats – and always, always, coming up against questions Ginger couldn't or wouldn't answer. Like who Susan was or what the fat little red notebook was for, or how he knew when Susan was calling him home.

"Why do you have a bluebird tattoo?" Laurie asked him one day.

"Don't you have one?" asked Ginger. "I think I was born with mine."

Ginger, to Laurie, was like one of those serials on television where you just *had* to see the next episode, only the next episode set up even more mysteries.

And of course the biggest mystery of all was the appearance of the Awesome Bird.

It first appeared in October, soon after the clocks had gone back an hour and it began to grow dark early.

Despite all the mysteries surrounding Ginger, Laurie might not have made any connection between bird and boy. He might have wondered, of course. Particularly hearing Ginger's fiddle at night, for Ginger's fiddle made you think he could call almost anything he wanted out of the sky.

But no, what made Laurie do more than wonder was the secret conversation he overheard between his mother and Susan.

CHAPTER 4

The Kiss of Life

It happened on a night when Laurie was keeping watch for the Awesome Bird.

He had seen it twice now, both times on a Friday night and he had told no-one. He wanted to make absolutely sure the bird wasn't a dream.

Sometimes, at breakfast, Laurie had told his mother the tale of a vivid dream. There'd been a dream about a man with wings on his feet and another about acrobats on the backs of bulls. The telling of such dreams usually meant camomile tea and early-to-bed. Dream or reality, Laurie had decided *not* to tell his mother about the bird.

And Ginger? Well Ginger, strange as he was, liked facts. Laurie needed to be certain the bird *was* a fact.

So that night, another Friday night, he had set his alarm for midnight and hidden it under his pillow. But what woke him up was not the haunting sound of the bird's wings flapping against the glass, or its beak's sharp tapping, or the great white spread of its feathers – but voices, raised voices from the sitting room. His mother's, anxious and angry, and another voice, quieter, more sing-song.

Laurie climbed out of bed and tip-toed to his door. It

was past eleven. Who was this late night visitor and why was his mother so angry?

"But why come *here*?" he heard his mother ask. The sitting room door was open but the other person was obviously sitting on the sofa, out of Laurie's sight.

Laurie crept out of his room and crouched down in the corner of the darkened hallway. Any sign of the visitor leaving and he could easily dash back into bed. But when the visitor next spoke, Laurie recognised her voice at once. And then he was glued there, in the hall's dark corner, wanting to hear every word. The visitor was Susan.

"You have to understand, Emily," said Susan, "that I can't just go where I choose. I'm given my instructions."

"But who gives them to you? And how?" asked Mrs O'Grady. (Laurie had never heard his mother sound so worried.)

"Emily, dear, you know I'm not at liberty to tell," said Susan. "As it is, you know more than you should. And that was only because you and Laurie appeared when you did – how many years ago? It must be ten now. And you were desperate for help. Simply desperate. Remember?"

"Of course I remember!" said Mrs O'Grady. "How could I forget? That remote road in the Scottish highlands. Not a soul in sight. Not a telephone kiosk for miles. The car in the ditch and Laurie . . . well, Laurie might not be here today if it hadn't been for you. So I'll always be grateful to you, Susan, but . . ."

"But you're worried about him," said Susan. "Worried about the kiss of life I gave him."

"Well," said Mrs O'Grady hesitantly, "not just the kiss . . . but what else you breathed into him."

"Don't think about it," interrupted Susan. "Laurie is a

perfectly normal eleven-year-old boy and likely to stay that way."

"Then how do you explain the vivid dreams he has – and his restlessness. Some days I think it's as if he doesn't really belong here."

"It will fade," said Susan. "Really, Emily, there are times I wish that I'd never told you anything about myself."

"You've never told me much," said Mrs O'Grady crossly. "All I've ever got out of you was that you were earth mother – a sort of foster mother – to children from some distant island. Children from 'There' was all you'd ever say. Children who were Dream-makers and Song-makers and stayed with you just long enough for them to understand the ways of the world. Children like Ginger."

Out in the darkness, Laurie listened with shivers running up and down his spine like light fingers up and down the keyboard of a piano, or Ginger's fast fingers on the frets of the fiddle. Fright and excitement were so mixed he couldn't tell one from the other.

"I wouldn't have told you that much if I hadn't thought it necesssary," said Susan. "I gave Laurie the kiss of life because there was no-one else there to do it . . ."

"And breathed into him – well, what can I call it? Something not quite of this world," said Mrs O'Grady.

"The Song," said Susan. "The Song of the Island."

"Whatever," said Mrs O'Grady wearily.

"You need never have known," said Susan beginning to sound cross too. "I don't suppose you'd have guessed. Laurie might have been dreamy from time to time and restless, perhaps. Or hungry for music and stories. But you wouldn't have known the difference. I did the only thing I could do. I couldn't give him life *without* the Song. I told you there was a danger. Small, but there."

"Things were getting better," said Mrs O'Grady. "Laurie hadn't mentioned any dreams. And he seemed more settled. But Ginger just wakened everything up in him. Yearnings. That's all I can call it. Yearnings for I don't know what."

"Probably for the Island," said Susan in a voice so low that afterwards Laurie wasn't sure he had heard it properly. "That will pass, Emily. Really it will. And Ginger hasn't got long now and then I'll be off . . ."

At this point Laurie's mother closed the sitting room door and the voices became an indistinguishable murmur.

Laurie crept back into bed and pulled the duvet tight about him. Even so it was a long time before he felt warm again, and even longer before he fell asleep.

What did it all mean? Sometime in the past – long ago and before Laurie could remember – he and his mother had known Susan. There had been an emergency. A road accident in Scotland. The accident in which his father had died and which Mrs O'Grady never talked about. And Susan had given him, Laurie, the kiss of life.

Laurie had read about the kiss of life. Ambulance men gave it to people who were nearly dying. If you did a course with the Red Cross you could learn how to do it so that if you were ever around when there was an accident and someone needed it, you could save them.

He'd have been a baby. Just about a year old. But it was more than the kiss of life that Susan had given him. She had breathed into him something from There, a song, a song from the Island of Dreams and Songs.

Was there, Laurie wondered, something now permanently wrong with him? Something which meant that he could never quite belong anywhere? Neither 'here' (so to speak) or 'there'? Or not until whatever Susan had breathed into him faded. But did he want it to fade?

If it was to do with dreams and islands and what his mother called 'yearnings', well, he didn't.

And what had Susan meant when she said Ginger didn't have long now? Long for what? The thought of Ginger leaving, just when Laurie had come to think of him as his best-friend-ever, gave Laurie an awful pain in his stomach. A mixed-up kind of pain, as you might try to mix two colours into one. There was a lonely pain and an angry pain and there was the pain of loneliness and anger fighting each other.

Laurie felt left out of everything. His mother and Susan had some secret from the past. Probably Ginger knew all about it – he seemed to know everything else. And anyway, Ginger was all right. Ginger, it seemed, was destined for adventures. He belonged to the Dream-and-Song-makers.

As soon as he thought this, Laurie knew exactly what his 'yearning' was for. More than anything else in the world he wanted to be in the place where dreams and songs were made. And added to all his other feelings about Ginger came a deep down squirmy (squirmy and squirly as the octopuses on the van) feeling of envy.

There was something else Laurie knew too as he lay sleepless in his bed. And it was about the bird. Whether it was a dream bird or a real bird, it came from There, from the Island of Songs and Dreams.

Laurie heard Susan leaving. The voices sounded happy now. Laurie heard his mother say, "You know I'll always care about you, Susan, wherever you are."

And he heard Susan's bright laugh, the laugh that often came when Ginger took up his fiddle. The laugh that warmed you right through. The laugh that turned into a dance.

"That goes both ways," said Susan.

Then the front door closed and Laurie heard his mother locking up and preparing for bed. Exhausted, he fell asleep himself.

* * *

All weekend Laurie said nothing. He knew, at heart, that he was sulking, but he couldn't help it. And on Saturday night, Sunday night and Monday night – three nights on the run, or on the wing – the bird appeared, its wings as luminous as moonlight itself.

Laurie got through Tuesday, through school and Scouts, like a zombie. He could think of nothing but the Island, the Song, the Bird. Then as if both the sulking and the fear lifted, simultaneously, like low clouds clearing, Laurie knew what he had to do. He took Puddles and went in search of Ginger.

CHAPTER 5

Secrets

"Describe it," said Ginger.

They were sitting on the embankment above the railway track – Ginger's favourite place. Puddles was investigating smells.

"It was enormous," said Laurie. "Its wings filled the whole window. And it seemed to want something . . . or someone."

"Did it have a heart-shaped face and hooded eyes?" asked Ginger.

"No," said Laurie. "It had a round face and your colour eyes. Conker brown. And its wings – they weren't *pure* white, they were flecked with all sorts of blues. The colours made me think of the most beautiful kind of marbles."

As usual Ginger had his red notebook with him and seemed to be making yet another list. He tapped his pencil on the page much like a doctor trying to work out what is wrong with a patient. "Did you see any ears?" he asked. "Short or long ears."

"I didn't notice any ears at all," said Laurie. "It was all sort of downy and beautiful. It made me think of mountains and seas."

"I suppose it didn't tu-wit, tu-woo?" asked Ginger hopefully.

"No," said Laurie. "It flapped and rat-tatted but it didn't tu-wit, tu-woo."

"It wasn't an owl," said Ginger decisively. "There are Tawny Owls and Barn Owls, Snowy Owls, Short- and Long-eared Owls and Little Owls. Your bird doesn't sound like any of them."

Ginger snapped shut his book and screwed up his face. He hated to be defeated by a question.

"I suppose it could have been a dream," Laurie said, all his old doubts coming back. "But I don't think so. You wouldn't dream the same dream so often, would you?"

"I never dream," said Ginger shortly.

"Never?" said Laurie astonished. "I thought everybody did. Perhaps you just don't remember."

"No," said Ginger in an end-of-conversation sort of way, "I just don't." And he opened his notebook again and began adding to his list. (It was trees today.)

Laurie felt very discouraged. All Ginger seemed to want was to collect as many facts as possible as fast as possible. You'd think he didn't have any feelings at all. He didn't seem to understand about the beauty – the mystery – of the bird.

"It would be a good sort of bird to have in your bird list," he said cunningly.

Ginger hesitated, tempted. "All right then. Shut your eyes and try and picture this bird again," he instructed.

Laurie obeyed. He could see the bird at once. Its wings were like two enormous finely ribbed fans.

"Well?" said Ginger. "Well?"

Laurie kept his eyes tight shut. "It's . . . it's . . . awesome!" he said. "Just awesome!"

And as soon as he'd said the word, he shivered all over. And when he opened his eyes Ginger had gone so pale that all his freckles stood out like currants in a bun, and he was shaking his head and thumping his ears with his hands.

"What's the matter?" asked Laurie.

"I don't know," said Ginger. "It was when you said awesome . . . I got a kind of echo in my head . . . like a sort of song."

Instantly Laurie was excited. This at least was some sort of clue. He clutched Ginger's arm.

"Ginger – Ginger, I know this might sound silly but do you think you've known me before? Known me in the past?"

Ginger shook off Laurie's hand. "Known you in the past? How could I?"

"It was just something I heard Susan say to my mum," said Laurie miserably.

"Susan's known a lot of children," said Ginger calmly. "I suppose you could be one of them."

"Why a lot of children?" Laurie jumped the question in fast before Ginger could go back to his tree list. Ginger was silent for a while then he said, "When you live with Susan, you don't ask things like that. There are just things you know and you don't know *how* you know them. Perhaps you were born knowing . . ."

Ginger stood up and began walking down the lane to the allotments. Laurie followed eagerly.

"Born knowing what?" he asked. "Do you know about There? Do you know about the Island – the Song-and-Dream-making Island?"

Ginger stopped in his tracks and again the same look came over his face as when Laurie had spoken of the

Awesome Bird. The same lost and unhappy look that turned Ginger so pale; Laurie thought he was going to be sick.

Then Ginger walked on, picking up a stick and whacking it against the fence of the allotments.

"I don't know anything about an island," said Ginger angrily. "Or about songs and dreams. And I don't want to know. I don't, don't, *don't* want to know!"

And with that he turned back and began running off towards the van.

"Susan's calling me," he shouted over his shoulder, although only someone with supersonic ears could have heard Susan calling, so Laurie knew Susan must be dancing and singing again.

"And I don't want to know anything about There!" Ginger shouted. "What I'm interested in is Here!" And he was gone.

Laurie and Puddles trailed miserably home. It had all gone horribly wrong, thought Laurie. At the very least he had expected Ginger to be interested in the Awesome Bird. And he'd hoped – *how* he'd hoped – that Ginger would share with him the secrets of the Island. For Laurie was convinced he knew. Why else should he turn so pale and ill when Laurie had spoken of both the Bird and the Island?

He knew all right. He was just holding out on him. Everyone was holding out on him. They were all keeping their secrets. His mother just wanted him to stay safely at home, all yearnings banished. And Ginger, whose life seemed as magical as his fiddle music, wanted to keep all that magic to himself.

Puddles rubbed himself against Laurie's legs. "Remember me?" asked his question mark.

Laurie reached down and patted him. But he'd made his decision. Next time the Awesome Bird appeared he was going to open the window and get out on the balcony and then . . .

Well, he had no idea what might happen, but it would be something extraordinary. Something awesome.

CHAPTER 6

Who is the Rabobab?

But it was another three difficult days and nights before the Awesome Bird appeared again. Laurie slept badly, couldn't concentrate at school – or even on his favourite television programmes. Mrs O'Grady began to suggest visits to the doctor, extra vitamins, camomile tea.

"You've got bags under your eyes, Laurie B," she said.

Every evening Laurie listened to Ginger's fiddle and stared up at the night sky – hoping. And the sound of Ginger's fiddle seemed to weave in and out of Laurie's dreams. On Tuesday night, Wednesday night and Thursday night, Laurie set his alarm clock (hidden under his pillow) for midnight. On Friday night, when the alarm gave out its muffled bleep, he was so tired that he groped under the pillow to switch it off and kept his head buried for several minutes.

It was only when, with a great effort, he opened his eyes and sat up that he saw it – the Awesome Bird – balanced on the railing of the balcony and staring in at him in a very patient way. The light cast by the Bird's bright white wings seemed to turn the whole room into a large milky pearl. It was almost as if the room itself had turned into the Milky Way – or how Laurie imagined the Milky Way might be.

Laurie slipped quietly out of bed. Even though he had been hoping for the return of the Awesome Bird, had been haunted by the memory of it and, indeed, had thought of little else, it was impossible not to be scared.

Laurie had often been scared. He'd been scared coming home in the winter dark when no-one seemed about and the trio of flats rose above him like grim giants. He'd been scared of Mr Littlewood, the maths teacher, who could throw a sudden temper and have you standing outside the headmaster's office before you had time to tighten your tie and tuck in your shirt. And when he'd first seen Susan dancing to Ginger's fiddle, he'd felt another kind of fear. The fear of something unexplained, unknown, uncanny.

From all these fears Laurie had learnt a few tricks of survival. (The Laurie B. O'Grady method of dealing with fright.) It helped, he discovered, to move very slowly and steadily and to do something ordinary like blowing your nose or tying your shoe-laces. It helped to think this was like a tunnel and you would be out of it soon. It helped to chant a rhyme or two.

So seeing the Awesome Bird curtaining his window with its bright spread of wings, Laurie stood for a moment in his T-shirt and underpants (he'd been sleeping in them so as to be ready) and then he said to himself.

"One, two three, Mother caught a flea,
Put it in a teapot and made a cup of tea."

Then he took a deep breath, pulled on his jeans and jersey, his socks and his slippers. Feeling slightly calmer he walked to the window, slid it open and climbed out on to the balcony.

The Awesome Bird waited – politely it seemed – clutching the railing with its bright yellow feet. Close up, Laurie could see that it had layers and layers and layers of feathers (rather like Susan's skirts and petticoats) of such soft snowy whiteness that they seemed as gentle as sleep itself.

The Bird tilted its head to one side and eyed Laurie as if waiting for something.

Laurie found himself wishing that Ginger was with him. Ginger would know what to do. Ginger would know how to address an Awesome Bird who visited you in the middle of the night. Did you shake a wing, for example, or maybe bow, or flap your arms as if they were wings too?

"Hello," said Laurie experimentally.

The Awesome Bird shifted its feet on the railings, fluffed its wings and waited.

"I'm very glad you've come," said Laurie politely. "I thought you might be a dream. I have a lot of strange dreams you know. There was one about acrobats and one about a man with wings on his feet and, well – I thought you were another. My mother gives me camomile tea. I don't know if you've ever tried camomile tea . . ."

Laurie stopped because of course the Bird could never have tried camomile tea or any other kind of tea. "I'm sorry," he said. "I'm prattling on, aren't I? That's what my mother calls it, prattling. Mr Littlewood says it's nerves. But you see I've never met an Awesome Bird before . . ."

The Awesome Bird raised one wing like the slow unfurling of a sail and gently brushed the top of Laurie's head.

"Oh!" said Laurie, and "Oh!" again, for the touch of the Bird's wing shivered all the way through him in a nice kind of sherberty-dip way, so that he felt all tingly afterwards – almost as if, he thought, he had just come alive.

Laurie shook himself, much like Puddles did when he'd been out in the rain. As if this was what he'd been waiting for, the Bird spread its wings. And at once Laurie knew what was wanted of him.

He felt perfectly calm now. The touch of the Bird's wing had worked like an enchantment.

"Just wait a minute," Laurie said, "I've got to write a note for Mum."

The Bird flapped a little, as if preparing for taking off. Hastily Laurie tore a piece of paper from his school Rough Book and found a biro.

Dear Mum, he wrote, and paused. (This wasn't an easy letter to write.)

I'm going off on an adventure. I hope you won't mind too much, but you see the Awesome Bird has come and I can't possibly say no. No to the Island, I mean. At least I think that's where we're going. I expect Susan and Ginger will know all about it.(Laurie paused again, changed his socks for clean ones and continued.) *The Awesome Bird seems very gentle and friendly – even though he is awesome. And I'm wearing my jeans and a jersey and my socks are clean. I am quite safe.* (Laurie underlined this twice). *Back soon.*

Love and hugs,

Laurie B.

He put the 'B' in because he thought his mother would like it – the down-to-earth B.

P.S. I think we are going to see the Rabobab.

When he had written this and put it on his pillow, Laurie stared at the note as if someone else had written it. Who was the Rabobab and how did he, Laurie, know that was where they were going? The name seemed to have popped up into his mind like toast popping out of a toaster. He thought of Ginger saying that there were some things you knew without knowing you knew them.

Outside, on the balcony, the Awesome Bird fluffed his feathers, impatient now.

"I'm coming! I'm coming!" whispered Laurie in case his mother should wake. And then on impulse he stuffed the biro and the Rough Book in his pocket, thinking of Ginger and the red notebook and how Ginger wrote everything down in it.

Wherever he was going and whoever the Rabobab was, he might well want to take notes, to report back as it were.

Climbing on the Awesome Bird's back, it never entered Laurie's head that there would be any difficulty about getting back. He felt as sure about it as if he had a return train ticket in his pocket. In fact the Rough Book seemed just that, a return ticket.

The Bird heaved a great soft sigh of relief when Laurie climbed on his back. The sigh bounced Laurie up and down and gave him time to burrow his hands deeply into the feathers round the Bird's neck and find a place to hold on to.

Even so, it was a rather bumpy take-off. They had to rise steeply over the flats and until they were over the city and up high with only cushions of clouds beneath them, the Bird seemed to find the flight hard work, as if the air currents were working against him.

At first Laurie prattled, and the fact that he didn't know if the Bird could either hear or understand him, made him prattle even more.

"This is the first Really Unexpected Thing that's ever happened to me," said Laurie. "You're more than Out-of-the-Blue, you're the first proper adventure that's come my way. Do we have far to go? Are we going to the Island? Are we going There? And who is the Rabobab?"

The Bird didn't answer of course. Its wings had found a

smooth and regular rhythm that gradually soothed Laurie into silence. He let his head sink into the soft warm feathers of the Bird's neck and then he slept.

In his sleep he thought he heard the Bird singing and the song somehow reminded him of Ginger's fiddle, only it was a sweeter, slower tune and although it had no words, Laurie knew it was the Song of the Island.

CHAPTER 7

A No-one from Nowhere

On and on flew the Awesome Bird until they were far away from the city, until they had left all land behind and were flying over the sea.

Laurie slept and woke, slept and woke. The song had stopped now and all Laurie could hear was the noise of the sea far below them, sounding like an orchestra of unknown instruments practising roars and hushes, swells and silences, and all he could see was the inky dark water beneath and the gleam of the Awesome Bird's outspread wings and the moon riding above them as if watching or following. It all seemed to go on for ever and ever, as if, thought Laurie, they were flying right out of time.

The Awesome Bird had gathered up speed now, the way a car does when released onto the motorway or a straight empty road. Despite the ins and outs of clouds, despite strong gusts of wind, the Awesome Bird flew smoothly and certainly.

In the sleeping patches Laurie dreamt of Ginger and Susan. He saw them in their van drinking mugs of tea and they seemed to be talking about him. Even in his dream Laurie wished he had a portable telephone so he could phone them up and say, 'Hello there! I'm on the back of the Awesome Bird heading for morning.' It would be better of course, to say 'I'm heading east, west, north or south,' but until the sun rose, Laurie wasn't quite sure which way they *were* heading.

In the waking patches, Laurie thought he heard the Song starting up again but he couldn't tell if it was the Bird singing, or a song that was in the air, or simply in his head. At any rate he felt he would soon know it off by heart and be able to whistle it. And because he was feeling a bit strange, lonely and homesick already, he thought how nice it would be to whistle it to his mum or to Susan and Ginger.

The Awesome Bird turned out to be very bad at landings. They bumped and tilted and dived downwards in a way that made Laurie feel very ill indeed. He had to clutch on tight to the Bird's neck feathers and shut his eyes to stop himself feeling sick and dizzy.

After a great many bumps and jolts the Awesome Bird skidded to a halt and Laurie fell off his back.

When he opened his eyes he found himself on a beach in bright, clear, early morning sunshine. The Awesome Bird had vanished and a girl of about his own age, with hair that was like a long black tangle of seaweed tied up with a piece of pink string, was looking down at him. She wore a pair of baggy shorts (tied round her waist with more pink string), a faded green vest and, Laurie saw, a bluebird exactly like Ginger's tattoed on the top of her arm.

"Oh dear," said the girl. "You aren't Ginger, are you?"

"No, I'm not," said Laurie rather crossly, for this wasn't much of a welcome. "I'm Laurie B. O'Grady."

The girl promptly burst into tears.

Laurie stood up and dusted the sand off himself. Above

him he saw dark cliffs and a narrow track winding round and up towards snowy-white cave houses set in the sides of the cliffs, and high above these what looked like the dome of a white palace.

He had no idea what to do. Girls – even ordinary ones at school – were an unknown quantity to Laurie and this one, who now sat sobbing on the sand, and sobbing very loudly, was a total conundrum.

Digging in his pockets Laurie came upon an ancient toffee.

"Would you like a toffee?" he asked, holding it out to the girl.

She stopped crying and took the toffee from him curiously. "What do I do with it?" she asked.

"You eat it, of course!" said Laurie, thinking at the same time that it was disconcerting to arrive somewhere where the inhabitants had never heard of toffees. It was not promising.

The girl unwrapped the toffee very carefully and nibbled a corner of it. "My name's Gwen," she said. "And this toffee is very nice. Have you any more?"

"No," said Laurie regretfully. "I suppose you couldn't tell me where I am, could you?"

"You're where you shouldn't be," said Gwen. "And that's Rabobab Island."

Laurie was tempted to say, well, hard cheese, because I *am* here and you'll just have to put up with me, but as there was no-one else to be seen and as he hadn't a clue about what to do next, he was anxious not to offend Gwen.

"I take it you don't like visitors," he said as politely as he could.

"We've never had one before," said Gwen.

37

"But you were expecting Ginger," said Laurie.

Gwen stared at him for a moment, her mouth glued up with toffee. "I suppose you can't help it," she said.

"Can't help what?" asked Laurie, exasperated.

"Can't help being so stupid. I've heard that's what Halvies are."

"Halvies?" echoed Laurie.

"Children who are half Rabobabs and half worldlings," said Gwen. "Halvies. I've heard stories about them, but I've never met one before. I always thought they stayed in the world but were song-haunted. It's all the fault of AB of course. Either he's in a sulk or he's not well. I'm not sure which. And nobody dares tell the Rabobab."

"AB?" queried Laurie.

"The Awesome Bird, of course," said Gwen with a toss of her seaweedy curls. "He's our messenger, you see, and the Rabobab simply adores him. Won't hear a word against him. And just lately AB keeps getting things wrong. Like you. His orders were to bring Ginger back."

Despite the bright sunshine, the stretch of beach that was like the Seaside of all Seasides, the curious cave houses with their bright blue doors and the road weaving invitingly up the cliffs, Laurie suddenly felt as if a great cloud of gloom had fallen on him.

He was the wrong one. The wrong boy in the wrong place. He was something called a Halvie. Someone who didn't belong here and didn't belong there.

Laurie stripped off his jersey. The sun was making its way up to the roof of the sky and, even without it, Laurie was feeling hot and bothered.

"You see," said Gwen, studying him. "You don't have the mark."

"What mark?" asked Laurie and there seemed to be so

many things he wasn't and so many things he didn't have that he quite despaired.

"Why the bluebird, of course," said Gwen showing off her own tattoo. "All Rabobab children have the mark of the bluebird."

Immediately Laurie remembered the bluebird on Ginger's arm. "Why do you have a bluebird tattoo?" he had asked. And then Ginger's light reply – "Don't you have one? I think I was born with mine."

"Perhaps I can get one," said Laurie hopefully. He had seen men with tattoos on their arms and hands – hearts and anchors, skull and crossbones, names. It couldn't be that difficult to get a bluebird tattoo and if it was painful, at that moment he was quite prepared to put up with the pain. Anything instead of being a Halvie, a no-one from nowhere.

"Maybe the Rabobab will give me one," Laurie continued. "Can you take me to see him, whoever he is?"

"Take you to see the Rabobab!" said Gwen and she laughed so much she fell over in the sand. "Nobody goes to see the Rabobab. Not unless He calls you to His presence."

"Well, how do I *get* called?" asked Laurie. He began to feel that Gwen was like the shop-keeper at the corner shop who always seemed determined not to be helpful and whatever you asked for he didn't have or couldn't get or had never heard of.

He could feel the tears smarting in his eyes and he turned away so that Gwen wouldn't see them.

Sitting in the sand, Gwen watched him for a time and then she said, "I suppose if you made up a perfectly splendid song, the Rabobab might summon you. It happens now and again."

Eagerly Laurie came and sat in the sand beside her.

"I could try," he said eagerly. "I could have a jolly good try."

Gwen considered him carefully and sighed. "I suppose now you're here," she said, "you'll have to be my friend instead of Ginger. I've been on the look-out for him for days."

"Well, I'm sorry," said Laurie, "not to be Ginger."

"That's all right," said Gwen, "I think you'll do. It could be quite fun changing you from a Halvie to a Rabobab child. But we'll have to keep it a secret at first. If the Rabobab did get to hear of you, or if anyone else guessed . . ." Gwen turned both her thumbs down.

"What?" asked Laurie, alarmed.

"Fade out," said Gwen. "And of course," she said casually, "if you do become a Rabobab child you couldn't go back. You'd be here for ever."

Laurie looked about him. It was all so beautiful. And there was that in the air that made you almost forget everywhere else; an exhilaration, a feeling of having arrived in paradise. To stay would be like being on holiday for ever, he thought. Who would want to go back to the greyness of Umberton Road, the flats, the boring old routine of school, Scouts, supermarket shopping?

He could play on the beach all day and every day. And when he wasn't doing that – well, there was the whole exciting mystery of making songs and dreams. Of course there was his mother, Susan and Ginger. Laurie pushed from his mind the feeling that perhaps he had stolen Ginger's adventure. What would happen to Ginger? Would the Awesome Bird go back for him? It was a question Laurie didn't want to ask. And then there was Puddles.

At the thought of Puddles Laurie got a lump in his throat, but he swallowed it down. He'd wanted excitement, hadn't he? Something different from the boring routine of life in Umberton Road. And now he'd got it. He'd found himself on the Island of Dreams. This is what he'd wanted – yearned for – wasn't it?

"Of course I'll stay forever," said Laurie.

"And be my friend?" said Gwen.

"Yes," said Laurie grinning.

Gwen held up the palm of her hand. "Pledge!" she said.

"Pledge!" said Laurie slapping her hand.

Gwen laughed. "Let's swim," she said. And the pair of them raced towards the sea.

★ ★ ★

Back in Umberton Road, a frantic Mrs O'Grady had just found Laurie's note.

CHAPTER 8

Mrs O'Grady in Dragon Mode

"It's all your fault, Ginger," shouted Mrs O'Grady, waving Laurie's note under Ginger's nose. "You and that fiddle of yours. You must have summoned this so-called Awesome Bird. Summoned him out of the sky. You and Susan – fiddling and dancing, making magic where magic shouldn't be."

Ginger was more than a little alarmed by the sight of Mrs O'Grady appearing at the door of the van first thing in the morning with her hair all sleep rumpled, and wrapped in a scarlet silk kimono complete with a dragon on the back. There were two sides to Mrs O'Grady – the pastel pink and blue side, and this scarlet side which, mostly, no-one saw.

"I don't know anything about an Awesome Bird," said Ginger miserably. "Or only what Laurie told me." As soon as he said the words, Ginger had to shut his eyes and shake his head for he heard the same singing as when Laurie had first mentioned the Bird.

Mrs O'Grady, hands on hips, eyed Ginger fiercely.

"And what, exactly, *did* Laurie tell you?" she demanded.

"Only that he'd seen one – or maybe dreamt one," said

Ginger, avoiding the words 'awesome' and 'bird'. "He asked me a lot of questions. Uncomfortable questions." Ginger wriggled both at the thought of Laurie's questions and under the fierce scrutiny of Mrs O'Grady's green eyes.

"Uncomfortable? Why uncomfortable?" asked Mrs O'Grady in the manner of a crime detective who regards even a wriggle as suspicious.

"Only that I didn't know any of the answers," said Ginger.

"So he told you he'd seen an Awesome Bird but he didn't tell you he was going to fly off on the back of one?" persisted Mrs O'Grady. "Is that it? And did he mention a Rabobab by any chance? Did he?"

"No," said Ginger, feeling now both miserable and guilty. "We've talked a lot about owls. At least I talked a lot about owls."

"Owls!" howled Mrs O'Grady. "Where is Susan? I have to see Susan at once."

Mrs O'Grady was now almost as scarlet as her kimono. It seemed to Ginger that she got redder and angrier by the minute and that at any moment fire might leap out of the dragon embroidered on the back of her gown.

"Susan's out," said Ginger. He wished he knew what to do with Mrs O'Grady. Whatever he said only seemed to make matters worse. And besides, the thought of Laurie going off on the back of the Awesome Bird had made him feel distinctly odd. He wanted to sit down in the quiet of the van and think about it. It was as if all this had happened before in another life that he couldn't quite remember.

"Out? This early in the morning?" shouted Mrs O'Grady as if this was another suspicious circumstance. "And why are you screwing your face up like that?"

"I was just trying to remember something," said Ginger apologetically. "And Susan's only gone for milk. She won't be long."

"Milk!" said Mrs O'Grady, plonking herself on the stool outside the van. "More like magic potions or spells to put ideas in the heads of people – to *breathe* into them!"

"Susan wouldn't do a thing like that!" protested Ginger, turning pink.

"Much you know about Susan," said Mrs O'Grady. "Or her powers. Well! I'm staying put until she comes back. Now you just go into that van and bring me all your books. There's got to be one about a Rabobab in there or I'm – I'm Father Christmas."

Ginger had to stop himself from grinning at this, for Mrs O'Grady, plump and round in her scarlet kimono, could, perhaps, have been a Chinese Father Christmas.

"But Mrs O'Grady, I don't think there *is* a book about the Rabobab . . ." Ginger began, and paused because the same dizzy, I've-been-here-before feeling came over him.

"No buts, Ginger," said Mrs O'Grady. "I know those books deal with magic crafts."

"But . . ." Ginger began again.

"Fetch them!" commanded Mrs O'Grady. "And while you're about it I'll have a cup of tea and a sandwich. Jam. I need sweetening up."

Laurie's disappearance had changed Mrs O'Grady from the nice, polite-but-distant woman who sometimes brought them soup or pots of jam or second-hand jerseys into someone fierce as the dragon on her kimono. Ginger wished she'd go home and put on something pale blue. But he hurried to obey. He hoped Susan would soon be back. He put on the kettle, piled a dozen books in a bag, dumped them at Mrs O'Grady's bare feet and went back in to make her a sandwich.

"I really think you must be imagining things," he said.

"*Me* imagining things!" shrieked Mrs O'Grady, waving Laurie's note under Ginger's nose. "I suppose this is an imaginary piece of paper, is it? I suppose I just imagined Laurie's bed was empty this morning and his window wide open and Laurie . . ."

And then to Ginger's horror, all the dragon went out of Mrs O'Grady and she began to cry.

"I'll make the tea," said Ginger quickly.

Mrs O'Grady dabbed her eyes and began looking at the books. They were a tatty pile, many of them dusty, dirty and torn. There were books with yellowing pages, books with pages missing, books with coffee or tea stains on their covers, or with old post-cards tucked inside them. There were books with names and dates scribbled inside them – 'To Amy on her 12th birthday with love from Dad, August 1923', read one. There was an old dictionary, two encyclopaedias, three anthologies of poetry, a book about the birds of Newfoundland, an English grammar, an adventure story called 'The Strangest Summer', a Greek phrase book, an atlas and a book of myths and legends.

Mrs O'Grady tried the dictionary for 'Rabobab', threw it aside and turned to the encyclopaedias.

Inside the van, Ginger spread two slices of bread with very thick blackcurrant jam (Mrs O'Grady's own, but he hoped she wouldn't remember) and added three spoons of sugar to the mug of tea. When he brought the tea and sandwich out to her, Mrs O'Grady had worked through the bird book (looking up both Awesome and Rabobab) and was going through the title page of a poetry anthology. There was nothing about a Rabobab.

Ginger set the mug and plate beside her and sat on the step of the van. Mrs O'Grady threw down the Greek phrase book which had no such useful phrases as 'Have you seen an Awesome Bird?' or 'Which way to the Rabobab?' in it.

"Ginger dear," she said (evidently much sweetened by the tea and sandwich), "did Laurie talk to you about this Rabobab? I need to know everything he said."

"But he never mentioned him!" said Ginger.

"Him!" pounced Mrs O'Grady. "The Rabobab's a 'him'?"

Luckily for Ginger, it was at this moment that Susan appeared. She came over the bridge singing and with her many petticoats bouncing in time to her song. The song stopped abruptly when Susan saw Mrs O'Grady and Ginger.

"Something's happened," said Susan handing Ginger the milk cartons. "What is it?"

Silently Mrs O'Grady handed over Laurie's note. Susan read it. Ginger took one look at Susan's face, fetched a deck chair and set it up. Susan sank into it. Her petticoats rose so high her face vanished behind them.

"That darn Bird!" said Susan. "I *knew* something had gone wrong. The messages have been muddled up for weeks now!"

Mrs O'Grady and Ginger stared at Susan open-mouthed.

"You *know* about the Bird?" they both said at once.

"Well, of course I know about the Bird!" said Susan.

Mrs O'Grady stood up. In the early morning light the silk of her scarlet kimono almost sizzled like sausages frying in the pan.

"Susan Smiley," said Mrs O'Grady. "It's time you told me everything."

CHAPTER 9

Rabobab 999

"I'm afraid we're in serious trouble," said Susan. "Ginger, go and make us some more tea and then you'd better go on a book hunt. This is not for your ears."

Ginger looked about to protest but Susan gave him a hug and pushed him gently into the van. "We'll need you soon enough," she said. Ginger brightened a little at the promise of being needed. He made them fresh mugs of tea, took his go-cart and went off over the bridge.

When he was out of sight, Susan heaved a sigh and said, "The Awesome Bird is the Rabobab's messenger. And you see he was *meant* to collect Ginger and take him back – back to the Island!"

Mrs O'Grady turned pale. Puddles drooped his ears. Even his question mark lost a little of its sharp enquiry.

"And instead he's gone off with my Laurie!" cried Mrs O'Grady. "Carried him off to this distant island of yours. This Island of Songs and Dreams, daffiness and dilliness!"

"Rabobab Island," said Susan, "to give it its proper name. I knew something had gone wrong because Ginger's time here is nearly up and usually a Rabobab child begins to get homesick for the Island. The Awesome

47

Bird pays a few preliminary visits and the child begins to remember the Island Song. It's called the Haunting Time. But it just hasn't happened."

"You mean it hasn't happened to Ginger," said Mrs O'Grady grimly. "It's my Laurie who's been haunted."

"I'm afraid so," said Susan. "And it's worse than that."

"Worse?" said Mrs O'Grady. "Can there be anything worse than having your son hi-jacked by an Awesome Bird?"

"The thing is," said Susan, "that Laurie must have been giving out blue."

"This is preposterous," said Mrs O'Grady. "What d'you mean, 'giving out blue'."

"It's a kind of aura," said Susan. "All Rabobab children have it. Like they all have the mark of the bluebird."

"There's no bluebirds on my Laurie," said Mrs O'Grady firmly.

"It goes back to the kiss," said Susan miserably.

"You told me it would fade!" said Mrs O'Grady accusingly. "You said the song would fade – pass away – Laurie would be a perfectly ordinary boy."

"I was wrong," said Susan. (All the warmth seemed to have gone out of her.)

"I thought because he was so small . . ."

"A babe . . . a mere babe . . . hardly one year old . . ." said Mrs O'Grady getting weepy again.

It was catching. Susan lifted the edge of one of her many skirts to wipe her eyes.

"Perhaps I should never have done it," she said.

"You had no choice," said Mrs O'Grady. "*We* had no choice. There'd be no Laurie at all if you hadn't given him the kiss."

"I spoke of a small danger . . ." said Susan.

Mrs O'Grady waited.

"And I'm afraid it's turned out to be a real danger. I think Laurie is what we called a Halvie."

Mrs O'Grady took an extra large gulp of tea as if this might bring things back to normal.

"A Halvie," she echoed. "It sounds like something you eat – like a Milky Way or a Mars Bar." Mrs O'Grady's voice rose an octave. "What on earth d'you mean, Susan – a Halvie?"

"A Halvie is a child who is half a worldly child and half a Rabobab child. There are a number of them. Some of them see the Awesome Bird by mistake and hear the song – and then they sort of catch it."

"Catch it?" repeated Mrs O'Grady hysterically. "You mean like measles or mumps or something?"

"Sort of," said Susan. "Once you've heard the Song it's almost impossible not to start dreaming of the Island. To have an inkling of another world. Of There. Sometimes you can see it in a child's eyes. He or she knows of the Rabobab."

Mrs O'Grady set down her mug and pulled her kimono tightly about her.

"Now just tell me, Susan – slowly please, because I can't quite take all this in – who or what is the Rabobab?"

"Please don't ask me that, Emily," begged Susan. "For I can't tell you without putting Ginger in great danger."

Mrs O'Grady was silent. Puddles put a paw on her knee. Mrs O'Grady held it absent-mindedly.

"All right, Susan," she said, "I won't ask you again who the Rabobab is, but it seems to me that my Laurie is in great danger and what I want to know is how we are going to get him back?"

Susan reached out and took Emily's hand. "What's

worrying me," she said, "is that Laurie might not want to come back."

"Of course he'll want to come back!" cried Mrs O'Grady, jumping up from her stool and stamping around the van. "Are you crazy? This is Laurie's home! This is where he belongs! He's got Puddles and me. He's Laurie B. O'Grady, just as I'm Emily B. O'Grady and Puddles is Puddles B. O'Grady."

"Yes, yes, I know," said Susan gently. "But you see the Island is very beautiful. It would be difficult for a child to be unhappy there. And besides the sea will slowly wash his memory away."

"You mean he'll forget us?" cried Mrs O'Grady. Puddles slumped to the ground. (Puddles could feel forgotten if you left him for half an hour!)

"He won't want to forget," said Susan. "But he won't be able to do anything about it. It takes about three days."

"Perhaps he'll stay out of the sea," said Mrs O'Grady. Susan shook her head. "Nobody could stay out of the sea on Rabobab Island," she said. "The Rabobab children often play in it all day. It's their element. And the sea is so clear and blue and warm that – well to ask a child *not* to swim in it would be like asking a bird not to fly or a mole not to dig or an elephant not to blow water out of its trunk."

Mrs O'Grady stood up and tied the belt of her kimono tightly about her like a soldier belting on his gun. Puddles stood to attention beside her.

"There's only one thing for it," she said. "We've got to go to Rabobab Island ourselves and get Laurie back. Laurie may have inklings and hauntings and all these other things you go on about, but home is where the heart is, and Laurie's heart is here, with Puddles and me."

"But there's only one way to get to the Island," said Susan. "And that's on the back of the Awesome Bird."

"Call him!" said Mrs O'Grady grandly. (She was back in dragon mode.) "Call him at once!"

"I'm afraid I can't do that," said Susan. "Either the Awesome Bird is sent. Or, in an emergency, a Rabobab child can call him."

"This *is* an emergency," said Mrs O'Grady. "So call him. Now."

"But I'm not a Rabobab child," said Susan. "I never have been. I'm like your Laurie. I'm a Halvie too. Many, many years ago, when I was a child, I saw the Awesome Bird. I was living, as you know, in the far north of Scotland and I think the Bird had got a little lost . . ."

"He seems to cause a great deal of trouble this bird," said Mrs O'Grady. "And if you want my opinion, he's not too efficient."

Susan ignored this and continued, "It was one of those very clear quiet moonlit nights. I don't know what woke me up. But I got out of bed and threw up my window, and I heard it. The Song. The Rabobab Song. We had a little croft far up in the hills. Probably the Bird thought no-one could hear him. But I did. I heard it all. And from that moment on – well, I suppose you could say I was enchanted. I leant out of my window and drank the Song in."

"And became a Halvie," said Mrs O'Grady.

"Yes," said Susan. "When the Rabobab heard of it, he decided I'd be an ideal foster mother for Rabobab children making their earthly visits."

"I can't think why they come at all," said Mrs O'Grady peevishly. "If the Island is as beautiful as you say it is."

"They have to learn earth ways and earth languages,"

said Susan, "so that when they are back on the Island they can make the songs and dreams to send back to us – songs and dreams we can understand. That's what it's all about. I mean where did you think songs and dreams came from?"

"I've never thought about it," said Mrs O'Grady crossly. "From our imaginations, I suppose."

"That's true, to a point," said Susan. "But our imaginations have to be fired or sparked. That's what the dreams and songs do. They come from outside time and they're always trying to reach us. What if there were no such things as dreams? What if we couldn't imagine what it was like to be an ant or an elephant? If we couldn't imagine what it was like to live two thousand years ago or how it might be to live in a future age?"

"I suppose it would be very dull," admitted Mrs O'Grady.

"And if we couldn't imagine finding a cure for cancer or discovering an unknown planet . . . ?" persisted Susan.

"If we couldn't imagine things . . ." said Mrs O'Grady very slowly. "Well, I suppose we'd be empty-hearted. Sort of – dead. Not quite human."

"And if," Susan continued gently, "I couldn't imagine how you were feeling now . . . ?"

"All right, all right!" said Mrs O'Grady, snappily. "There'd be no love. Satisfied?"

Susan grinned. "Well, now you know why making songs and dreams is terribly important work," she said.

"Yes," said Mrs O'Grady. "But there's something *you're* forgetting Susan. It seems to me that Laurie has terribly important work to do now here on earth. It's called growing up. And to do that he needs two feet on the ground. This ground. So how *are* we to call up this Awesome Bird?"

Susan was silent for such a long time that Mrs O'Grady shook her, thinking she had fallen asleep.

"Ginger," said Susan. "Only Ginger can do it."

"Well, call him at once, woman!" cried Mrs O'Grady. "What are we waiting for?"

"It will be a great shock to him," said Susan.

Mrs O'Grady went into another sizzle of scarlet outrage. "A shock! A shock!" she cried. "What sort of shock do you think I had this morning? There I am, armed with a cup of tea, going to wake Laurie up and what do I find? His bed empty and this note – this crazy, crazy note all about Awesome Birds and Rabobabs. I'll give you shocks, Susan Smiley. Just get Ginger here and fast."

"You see Ginger doesn't *know* he's a Rabobab child. Just as on the Island the sea washes away the memory of the time on earth – so a Rabobab child forgets all about the Island during his flight here. And he only begins to remember very slowly at the Haunting Time. After about five months, he or she feels the call of the sea. The bluebird tattoo starts to ache a little and so does the child's heart. And then the Awesome Bird appears, just as a gentle reminder. Then one day the child wakes up and says, 'I think it's time to go home.'

"If things are going to plan, the Awesome Bird usually comes within the week and off the child goes. And I move on. Wait for the next child. A Rabobab child who isn't quite ready to go back to the Island can often become quite ill."

"We'll have to risk that," said Mrs O'Grady. "It seems to me that there's a far greater risk of my losing Laurie altogether."

"Yes," said Susan. "I suppose you're right. We'll have to put the emergency call into action."

"What's the emergency call?" asked Mrs O'Grady. "Do you have some kind of Rabobab 999?"

Susan ignored the sarcasm. "Really it's only meant to be used if a Rabobab child is in danger," said Susan. "Then he sings a special song of his own and the Awesome Bird hears it and comes at once. It's known as the High-Pitched Yodel."

"And does Ginger know it?"

"Oh every Rabobab child knows it," said Susan. "Ginger was born knowing it. But he doesn't as yet *know* he knows it."

"Well, you'd better tell him," said Mrs O'Grady. "We can't hang about here much longer. Goodness only knows how long Laurie has spent in the sea by now and how much memory has washed off him."

"I'll call Ginger," said Susan.

Mrs O'Grady watched as Susan began to dance. It began as quite a slow dance and involved much swirling of Susan's petticoats and a great deal of stamping. Mrs O'Grady wondered if Susan's stamping sent some kind of tremors under the earth which in some magical way reached Ginger's feet. Or if, perhaps, Ginger had extra special hearing and could hear the stamping from miles away. When the dance was really under way Susan began singing.

Mrs O'Grady couldn't understand the words although every now and again she thought she heard the word 'blue' and the word 'sea'.

Puddles cheered up a lot when he saw Susan dancing and attempted to join in. His ears had perked up and folded on top of his head like a bow and he chased his tail faster and faster in a way that made Mrs O'Grady quite dizzy to watch.

Very soon she heard the squeaky wheels of the go-cart and the next minute there was Ginger, trundling over the bridge.

Mrs O'Grady had never been so pleased so see anyone in her whole life.

CHAPTER 10

The Sea of Forgetting

Laurie swam in his underpants, throwing off his T-shirt and tugging off his jeans as he and Gwen ran down the beach and into the bouncy, springy waves. They were the sort of waves that lifted you up on their backs and then slid you down the other side. Gentle bucking-bronco sort of waves that you jumped on and rode and then fell off into the blue duvet of sea before the next wave came rushing in with an I'm-coming-I'm-coming-I'M COMING to lift you up in its swooping arms.

The water was warm as a bath and so clear that Laurie could see down to the sand underneath, to where the pink seaweed like very tiny trees spun by spiders, rocked and shivered.

Laurie felt as if every bit of him was suddenly free. It wasn't just that he could kick and splash, leap and flop, lie on his back and float – it was as if the sun beating on the sea sent sparks flying such as a blacksmith might make hammering out silver, and the sparks and glints of sunlight were like micro-chips of magic stinging him with happiness, scrubbing him with energy, rubbing him down with sunshine.

Gwen was a far stronger swimmer than Laurie. She had

sped out towards the horizon doing the crawl. Laurie could see the flash of her elbows and behind her, like the gleaming wonder of a mermaid's tail, a wake of silver-shining foam.

When she came back to him, her black seaweedy tangle of hair was plastered flat on her head and her face shone with water.

"This is marvellous!" Laurie gasped. He was out of breath with diving under and over the waves.

Gwen laughed back at him, dived under the water, tickled his feet and came up spluttering.

"This will wash all your worries away," said Gwen.

"It certainly will!" agreed Laurie.

"We call it the Sea of Forgetting," said Gwen.

Laurie stopped wave-leaping and doggy-paddled as fast as he could. "What do you mean, the Sea of Forgetting?" he asked.

"Well, just that," said Gwen. "The past is washed away. If you were Ginger, your memory would be handed in to the Book-Keeper . . ."

"The red notebook," spluttered Laurie getting a mouthful of water.

"Yes. Your memory," said Gwen bouncing quite happily up and over a wave. "And then you'd wash away all knowledge of your time on earth by swimming in the Sea of Forgetting and after that . . ."

But Gwen didn't have time to say what came after that because Laurie was wildly splashing and scrambling back to the shore.

Gwen followed more slowly, shaking herself like Puddles did on the rare occasions when he was given a bath, and wringing her hair out like a dish cloth. When she reached Laurie he was sitting on a rock, drying himself with his T-shirt and talking to himself out loud.

"I live in Flat 6, Block B, Clampitt Court, Umberton Road, Rodwell, England, The World," he said. "I live in Flat 6, Block B, Clampitt Court, Umberton Road . . ."

"Is this a sort of song?" asked Gwen, gazing at him astonished. "What on Rabobab are you going on about."

"Remembering," said Laurie briefly. "I live in Flat 6, Block B . . ."

Gwen groaned and flopped on the sand beside him. "Forgetting doesn't work *that* quickly," she said. "Time is quite sticky. It will take about three days before you're clean of sorrow."

"Is that what you call it?" asked Laurie. "Forgetting the past."

"Of course," said Gwen. "It's beautiful here and all the Rabobab children are happy. Apart from the time when we're busy making dreams and songs, we're free to swim and play. Every night we're washed in the light from the Lighthouse and every day we wash off the past in the sea. What do you want to remember for?"

And Gwen had painted such a happy picture of life on the Island that Laurie found it hard to answer. Remembering seemed important, but he couldn't say why. "I just do," he said sulkily.

"You just do! You just do! You just do!" taunted Gwen dancing about him. "I think you're very, very stupid. Ginger would never be so stupid!"

Laurie was so angry he forgot that Gwen was the only person he knew on the Island and that he was totally dependent on her help.

"Don't call me stupid," he said. "That's what my mother calls me when she thinks I haven't been listening properly."

Gwen stopped in the middle of her prancing and gazed

at Laurie as if he'd suddenly grown an extraordinary nose or purple ears.

"You have a mother?" she said.

"Of course I have a mother," said Laurie irritably. "Everyone has a mother. I have my mum and Puddles and we live at Flat Number 6, Block B, Clampitt . . ."

"Don't start that all over again," begged Gwen, squatting beside him. "Tell me about mothers."

And now it was Laurie's turn to be astonished.

"Well what do you want to know?" he asked. "You must know about mothers from your own mother."

"We're children of the sea," said Gwen. "We just have the Rabobab and the Caretakers. Of course I've *heard* about mothers. When a Rabobab child comes back from the world he or she sometimes talks about the mother. The funny thing is, mothers seem hard to forget . . . mothers seem to be the stickiest things of all."

Laurie thought of Susan and how much she loved Ginger and how awful it would be if Ginger were to forget her.

"What else does your mother say," asked Gwen. "I want to know everything."

Laurie thought hard. "She says, 'Don't make a fuss'," he said, "And 'Don't forget your homework', and 'Don't leave your bedroom in a mess'."

"What a lot of don'ts," said Gwen and she began dancing about on the beach singing,

"Don't make a fuss, fuss, fuss.
Don't make a mess, mess, mess."

Laurie watched her. He wished Ginger was here with him. You could have a decent conversation with Ginger.

"Do shut up!" he cried. "You're really getting on my nerves!"

Gwen stopped in mid-song and dance and glared at him, tossing her seaweedy hair.

"All right, Laurie B. Halvie," she said. "I'll stop. You can find your own way." And she began marching off up the beach.

"But where am I to find my own way *to*?" Laurie shouted after her.

Gwen didn't answer.

"I don't think much of your Rabobab Island," Laurie shouted. "Not if you're a typical Rabobab child."

Gwen paused and looked over her shoulder at him. "You find your way to the Palace of Songs and Dreams, of course," she said.

"But what do I do when I get there?" called Laurie.

"Find out for your stupid self!" shouted Gwen and disappeared up the path.

Laurie sat down in the sand again. How odd it was, he thought, to feel unhappy in such a very beautiful place. He had been so carried away by the sea and the sunshine and swimming that he hadn't really looked about him.

Now he did. There was the narrow track up the dark cliffs and the snow-white cave houses all with identical blue doors set into the side of the cliffs. Sort of like the flats, thought Laurie and felt vaguely comforted.

The beach formed a bay and when Laurie looked up to the top of the cliffs he could see three larger buildings. Where the cliffs jutted out over the sea, stood what was obviously the Lighthouse that Gwen had spoken of. Highest of all was what looked like a distant tower and between the tower and the Lighthouse, he could just about see a white dome. Was this the Palace of Songs and Dreams? Or maybe the Palace of the Rabobab? Perhaps the cave houses were all a part of the Palace and it was just a question of finding the entrance.

One thing was certain. He was in for a long, steep, daunting climb. For the first time Laurie wondered just *how* he would get home if he wanted to – not that he did, of course.

This was an adventure, wasn't it? And no-one expected an adventure to be easy. And why was he bothered about forgetting? Maybe Gwen was right and it was good to wash away the past. Maybe memories weighed you down . . . yet somehow they were *his* memories and he didn't want to let them go.

With a rather heavy heart Laurie pulled on his jeans, his damp T-shirt and his very silly slippers and began walking up the steep path.

CHAPTER 11

Finnegan's Whiskers

"I suppose I just ask the first person I see," Laurie said to himself as he began climbing. Only there didn't seem to be anyone about. Perhaps they were all busy singing and dreaming.

Laurie realised, as he trudged up the path, his slippers flapping, that he was both tired and hungry and that it was an awfully long time since he had eaten anything. In fact he had no idea what time it was at all – other than long past breakfast. *Did* you eat in the Palace of Songs and Dreams or did you feed on moonshine and rainbows? Laurie very much hoped not. His own dream right at that moment was of sausages, bacon and toast. Lots and lots of toast.

Apart from the shushing of the sea below him, the Island seemed completely silent. Laurie was very glad indeed when he heard the sound of trotting hooves and someone singing and when he turned the first corner he saw that the singer rode a donkey. It was a very sturdy donkey with a bright yellow blanket under the saddle and red and yellow bobbles bouncing on its forehead.

Its rider was all round. Round cheeks, a rounded tum and bum, two round saddle-bags slung on either side of the donkey – even the song he sang seemed to be rounded for it rolled on and on in a non-stop kind of way so that when the man got to the end of it, he went straight back to the beginning.

"There was a man called Michael Finnegan,
He grew whiskers on his chin again,
The wind came out and blew them in again,
Poor old Michael Finnegan, begin again,"

he sang.

Laurie, who might have politely waited for a pause in the song, realised that there wasn't going to be one and that the singer was so carried away with himself that he would have to interrupt. So before the wind could blow Michael Finnegan's whiskers in again, Laurie called out, "Excuse me! I say, excuse me! Can you tell me the way to the Palace of Songs and Dreams?"

The man was so surprised by this interruption that he almost fell off his donkey.

"I'm sorry to stop you in mid-song," said Laurie, "but I'm looking for the Palace of Songs and Dreams and I don't know if I should head for the dome or the tower and there aren't any street signs or any numbers on the houses and it's very muddling when *all* the doors are blue and . . ."

To his horror, Laurie found he was crying.

The man rolled off his donkey and came to sit at the side of the path beside Laurie. Laurie saw that even his knees were rounded and the toe caps of his bright blue boots.

"But *is* there any colour for doors apart from blue?" he asked.

"Well, at home, we have all colours," Laurie began.

"My own front door is . . . is . . ." and suddenly he found he couldn't remember what colour it was.

"At home?" questioned the man. And then he slapped one round knee and said, "I've got it! You're just back from WW, aren't you?"

"WW?" said Laurie.

"The Worldly World," said the man.

"Oh, of course. Yes, I am," said Laurie nervously.

The man scratched his round bald head. (It was a little as if he couldn't manage whiskers on his chin *and* hair on his head.)

"Funny," he said, "I thought you had ginger hair. But I often get things wrong. It's going round and round that does it. I'm Michael Finnegan."

"The *real* Michael Finnegan?" asked Laurie.

"Is there another one?" asked Finnegan.

"Well, I thought Michael Finnegan was just a person in a song," said Laurie.

"So he is," said Michael Finnegan. "It's my song. And if you are about to suggest that I am not a real person but just an imaginary one in a song, then I'll say good-day to you."

"No, no, I'm quite sure you're real," said Laurie. "There's so much of you."

Michael Finnegan gave a great round roar of laughter and slapped his thighs one after the other.

"All right then," he said, holding out a large round paw. "We're friends then, you and I. Perhaps life in the WW has changed your ginger hair? Turned you mouse."

"Perhaps," said Laurie cautiously.

It was tempting to tell Michael Finnegan everything because he was so round and friendly, but Laurie hesitated. He was glad his T-shirt had short sleeves or

Finnegan might have noticed the lack of the bluebird tattoo.

"Well, no matter," said Michael Finnegan, "How can I help you."

"I seem to have forgotten the way to the Palace," said Laurie.

Michael Finnegan nodded. "It sometimes happens when children first return," he said. "Memory muddle. Changing one life for another and all that."

"Tell me," said Laurie – for this seemed a safe question to ask – "if I swim in the sea will I forget everyone at . . . down in WW?"

Michael Finnegan regarded him silently for a long moment so that Laurie began to wonder if it was quite such a safe question after all.

"Time washes off you in the sea," said Finnegan. "But love doesn't."

"Oh good," said Laurie before he could stop himself. "That means I won't forget my mum and Puddles," and then he clapped his hand over his mouth.

But Michael Finnegan made no comment. "Come on," he said, standing up and climbing back on his donkey. "I'll give you a lift to the Palace. Could have sworn you had ginger hair."

Laurie said nothing. He clambered up on the donkey's back and put his arms round Finnegan's round waist.

"Heigh up!" said Finnegan, slapping the donkey's rump and with a toss of its head the donkey began clopping up the steep cliff path.

It seemed that Michael Finnegan couldn't ride without singing, so sing he did, with his whiskers going in and out at the right moments in a way that was quite disconcerting and which also made it impossible to talk to him.

But Laurie didn't mind. It gave him a chance to look about him. The Island seemed to be coming to life now. Rabobab children, appearing out of the blue doors, began running up the path. They were very nimble, Laurie noticed, and a lot of them had hair like Gwen's. A few had Ginger's ginger hair. They wore a rag-bag of shorts and vests as if each child had just grabbed whatever was nearest to hand, no matter what size. There were so many bluebird tattoos flashing about on bare arms that Laurie thought he'd get spots before his eyes if he kept on looking.

"Snooze Hour is over," said Finnegan, between rounds of his song, and Laurie realised that it must be late afternoon and that he'd heard how, in hot climates, people had a siesta in the heat of the day. A snooze hour must be the same thing.

The Palace of Songs and Dreams turned out to be the large domed building Laurie had seen from the shore. It was right on the very top of the cliff and now that they were up there, Laurie could see that the Lighthouse, on the cliff's edge, was not as far away as it appeared from the shore.

The donkey stopped outside the Palace without being told and Michael Finnegan finished his song at 'Poor old Michael Finnegan' and didn't begin again. Laurie was rather relieved. The song was going round and round in his own head.

"Here we are then," said Finnegan, rolling off the donkey and helping Laurie down.

Laurie looked up at the Palace. "Does the Rabobab live here?" he asked.

Michael Finnegan looked quite shocked. "Oh dear, you *do* have memory lag," he said. "No, of course not. Oh well, I expect it will all come back to you soon. You won't have forgotten Janni Bean will you?"

"Janni Bean?" repeated Laurie.

"The finest cook that ever there was," said Michael Finnegan.

"Of course," said Laurie hastily.

"Well, I must be on my way," said Michael Finnegan climbing up on his donkey again.

"Are you going so soon?" asked Laurie, for he had been hoping Finnegan would come with him into the Palace.

"Of course," said Finnegan. "Got to be on my rounds you know. That's what I do, you see. Go round in circles." And he roared with laughter. "I'll see you later," he cried as the donkey began trotting down the path. Laurie could hear the song disappearing into the distance.

He stood and studied the Palace. It was a large square building, with the dome set on it like a round sun hat on a big white box.

The strangest thing about the Palace was that it was surrounded by tall silver poles. The finest of wires ran between them (so that Laurie was reminded of the five lines on a stave of music) and the wires ended in strange little curly spirals, some short, some long but all bouncing in the gentle wind. The wires hummed and trembled, some with a low vibrating sound, some with a high fine single note, others with a kind of jingle.

The entrance to the Palace was far from grand. Indeed it reminded Laurie of the swinging doors he'd seen in cowboy films. He soon realised the reason for this. The doors were very easy for the Rabobab children to rush in and out through, which a large number of them were doing.

Laurie stood in the hall for a moment wondering which

way to go next, wishing that either Gwen or Michael Finnegan were with him. And then he smelt it. Toast!

Janni Bean, Laurie said to himself, the finest cook that ever there was. And he followed his nose down a long corridor of what seemed to be music studios – for he could hear all kinds of songs being rehearsed over and over, while the smell of toast grew mouth-wateringly nearer. At last, at the very end of the corridor he found the kitchen.

It was a vast kitchen, certainly as large as the whole of Flat 6, Block B, Clampitt Court and maybe number 7 too. There was a huge oven at one end which consisted of a large steel box with hobs on the top, and a roaring fire beneath it. A great range of pans and pots of all shapes and sizes bubbled on the hobs and a large hammock hung from the ceiling as if these pots and pans needed watching over throughout the night.

On the kitchen table was an enormous silver toaster that toasted ten slices at once and standing beside it, actually standing on the table dunking a burnt slice in a bucket of water, was Janni Bean the best cook that ever was known.

Janni Bean was about the same height as Laurie but she was straight and boney in all the places Michael Finnegan was plump and round.

"You're late!" said Janni and she pressed the button on the toaster so that all the pieces jumped out together. "Catch!" she cried. Laurie managed to catch two and Janni, laughing, caught the other eight, much like a juggler catching clubs. As Laurie stood there, his mouth open in astonishment, Janni climbed down on to a stool and began buttering.

"Sit yourself down," she said pointing to another stool and putting before him a plate piled with eight buttered slices. There was something curiously familiar about the plate with its pattern of swirly blue octopuses round the rim.

Hands on her hips, Janni watched him. "It is the right plate, isn't it?" she asked.

"It's just like Susan's," said Laurie.

"Well, you're allowed a few WW comforts on your first day back," said Janni. "While you're still heavy with time."

"I don't feel heavy," said Laurie. "I feel rather light. I think I must have lost about a stone in weight just getting here and waiting for breakfast."

"Breakfast!" said Janni. "You *are* out of sync. This is more like tea."

"How did you know I was coming?" asked Laurie through a mouthful of the most wonderful toast he'd ever tasted.

"You're in the book, of course," said Janni.

"The book?" asked Laurie.

"Why the Book-Keeper's book, of course," said Janni. "What a memory muddle you're in!" And Janni walked carefully round him three times. "Ummm," she said after a long pause. "You're not very ginger are you, Ginger. Didn't they give you enough marmalade down there."

Laurie almost choked over his toast. "I think I've faded," he said. "Down in WW. Yes, that's it. I've faded."

"Poor dear," said Janni sympathetically. "It had better be carrots and marmalade for a while then."

"Perhaps it had better," said Laurie miserably, for there were such wonderful smells coming from Janni's various pots and pans that the thought of a diet of carrots and marmalade sounded extremely dull.

"Or ginger cake," said Janni.

"Yes," said Laurie more enthusiastically. "Ginger cake might do it."

"In the circumstances," said Janni, "you'd better have a piece or two now."

She took down a tin the size of a car wheel, rolled it out on the table and cut Laurie a large slice.

By the time he had finished the second slice, Laurie was so tired he could hardly keep his eyes open.

"You look as if you've had a very hard time down in WW," said Janni. "Or did Awesome Bird give you a rough ride?"

"It was a little bumpy," said Laurie.

"Uummm," said Janni again. "Well, I think no beach-sleep for you tonight. You're probably not up to it. You can sleep in the hammock and report to the Book-Keeper tomorrow."

Laurie didn't have the courage to ask her where he would find the Book-Keeper or quite what he had to do or say when he did find him. And what did she mean by beach-sleep?

Well, any kind of sleep would do at the moment, and when Janni dropped down the hammock, Laurie stood on the kitchen table and climbed into it. Janni covered him with a blanket and, small as she was, hauled the hammock up again so that Laurie hung from the ceiling, rocking gently.

Dozens of muddled thoughts swam sleepily in his head. Would he find Gwen again? What would happen to Ginger, left down in the WW? How much time had already washed off him? So far, he thought, both Michael Finnegan and Janni Bean seemed to believe he was a true Rabobab child. But what would happen if they discovered he was only a Halvie? Not Ginger at all, but Laurie B. O'Grady. Laurie B. Halvie.

Still, there were the songs and dreams to find out about and his tale of having faded was a bit of a master-stroke. Laurie giggled.

"What's the joke?" Janni called up.

But there was no answer. Laurie was asleep.

CHAPTER 12

♫

Always Attend to Shivers

"You'd better sit down, Ginger," said Susan. "There are things I have to tell you."

The morning had darkened. They had all gone inside the van and Susan had lit the oil lamps. They sat on the bunks around the table-built-on-books.

"Things you need to be told, and things we need you to do," said Mrs O'Grady.

"Give the boy a chance, Emily," said Susan sharply. "Tell me, Ginger, when you hear about the Awesome Bird, do you remember anything?"

"I don't exactly remember," said Ginger. "But when Laurie first spoke of him – and when you did – well, it's as if I can hear a song in my head. A song I once knew."

Ginger looked from one serious face to the other. There was a look on Susan's face that he'd never seen before. A look which made him afraid, so that for the first time he felt forced to ask the question he had long wanted to ask, but, for fear of the answer, never quite dared.

"Susan, are you my mother?" asked Ginger.

To his horror Susan, Susan Smiley, *his* Susan Smiley, wiped away a tear and said, "In a manner of speaking I'm your mother, Ginger. Yes, in a manner of speaking . . ."

and she gave him a big hug, or a hug that was big for such a small person as Susan.

But the hug didn't cheer Ginger much. What did Susan mean by 'in a manner of speaking'. Either she was his mother, or she wasn't. There was no 'manner of speaking' about it.

Susan fixed her eyes intently on Ginger. "That song you say you can hear in your head," she said. "That's the Song of Rabobab Island."

When she said the word 'Rabobab', Ginger felt a kind of tug at his heart. It was the same kind of tug he felt in his feet when Susan danced the homing dance, only this was more painful. It almost made him feel faint.

Susan leant forward and took his hand. (Mrs O'Grady tapped her feet impatiently.)

"I think you know the truth really, Ginger," said Susan. "When I said I was your mother in a manner of speaking, I meant I was your earthly mother, but really . . ." Here Susan paused, for it was Ginger's turn to cry and Susan dabbed at his freckled cheeks with her large blue hankie. "Really, you're a Rabobab child. You belong to the Island."

"Then why did the Awesome Bird take Laurie, not me?" asked Ginger. "Is Laurie a Rabobab child too."

"Certainly not!" said Mrs O'Grady.

Susan hushed her with her hand. "This is all a great shock to Ginger," she said. "He's meant to recover his memory gradually. Not all at once, like this. Homesickness is something that's meant to ripen slowly, like a plum."

Mrs O'Grady hushed.

Susan pulled out a rug from a shelf above the bunk and tucked it round Ginger. Mrs O'Grady made him hot chocolate. (She needed Ginger on her side.)

"Unfortunately," said Susan as Ginger sipped his chocolate and began to look more like Ginger again, "the Awesome Bird has made an awful mistake. He's the Rabobab's messenger, as you know. And he should have taken you. He took Laurie instead."

"I'm awfully sorry, Mrs O'Grady," said Ginger.

"It's not your fault," Mrs O'Grady admitted reluctantly.

"It's all beginning to come back to me now," said Ginger. "The Island, and how beautiful it is, and how happy the children are, and the sea and the Palace. Susan, were you once a Rabobab child?"

Susan shook her head. "No," she said. "I'm like Laurie. I'm what's called a Halvie – we're people who belong to two worlds. You could say we're not quite Here and not quite There!" And Susan laughed, wistfully.

Mrs O'Grady sniffed.

"There had to be somewhere for the Rabobab children to come when they visited here," continued Susan, "and someone who knew about the Island, and so I volunteered. I got the van because when a Rabobab child lands – and it can be anywhere – he comes in a kind of parachute shawl and stays asleep in it for five or six hours. When he wakes, well, he thinks he's always lived with me."

"But don't you miss the Island?" asked Ginger, and as he asked he knew exactly what the tug at his heart had been. The Very Homesick tug.

"I've only been there once – years and years and *years* ago – and since then, well the children keep me warm."

"Keep your sunshine," suggested Ginger.

"Yes, keep my sunshine," agreed Susan. "But now I think you're missing the Island aren't you, Ginger?"

"Yes," said Ginger. "Now that I've remembered, it's given me an ache."

Susan nodded. "It's time for you to go," she said.

"And time for Laurie to come back," said Mrs O'Grady.

Puddles, curled up in front of the wood-burning stove, thumped his tail at the mention of Laurie.

"That's where we need your help, Ginger," said Susan.

"You've got to call up that foolish Bird," said Mrs O'Grady.

"I don't think it's a good idea to call him foolish," said Susan.

"All right. You've got to call up that wondrous, awesome amazing Bird who's behaved in this perfectly ridiculous manner," said Mrs O'Grady.

"Emily wants to go to Rabobab Island and rescue Laurie," said Susan.

"I've been patient enough," said Mrs O'Grady. "And I'm not going to sit here and wait for Laurie to drop out of the sky. Or trust to that Bird to bring him back."

"Is it allowed," asked Ginger, "for a worldly mother to go to the Island?"

"I don't care whether it's allowed or not . . ." began Mrs O'Grady.

Susan hushed her again.

"I don't know if it's even possible," she said. "But it certainly isn't without your help, Ginger."

"What do I have to do?" asked Ginger.

"Do you remember the High-Pitched Yodel?" asked Susan.

"The emergency call-out song?" said Ginger.

"Yes," said Susan.

"I'm not sure," said Ginger, screwing up his face. "I seem to know things I didn't know I knew. I just get a shiver."

"Always attend to shivers," said Susan. "Shivers tell you things. Try and remember."

"Yes, try!" said Mrs O'Grady urgently.

"I need to be outside," said Ginger.

They followed him out of the van. Still wrapped in the rug, Ginger stood with his eyes shut. Puddles lay flat on the ground as if he knew something strange was about to happen. Ginger's face seemed to change as they watched him. It seemed rounder and more peaceful. Ginger even smiled.

And then he began the High-Pitched Yodel.

It was the most incredible sound you ever did hear. It was so high, that up in the flats light bulbs exploded and glasses twanged into pieces. Windows were flung open. Faces gazed out. Ginger's song rose up in the morning air as if he was singing in a cathedral.

It was such a high, slow, bird-like yodel that the clouds above them seemed to stir and part. Susan and Mrs O'Grady found themselves staring upwards. Ginger stood between them, his hair suddenly sharply bright, his eyes tight, his skinny little self tense with concentration. It was as if each note of the song had to be brought up from some deep down memory within him. Mrs O'Grady pressed her hands to her mouth to stop herself shouting out loud. Puddles crawled under the van.

As they stared upwards at the drifting, parting clouds, they saw a shape. At first it was hard to distinguish from the clouds, then as it came lower and lower it became recognisably Bird. Awesome Bird. They saw the gleam of its aquamarine wing tips; fine edging feathers which looked as if they had been dipped and dyed in the sea. They saw its dazzling whiteness.

Susan and Mrs O'Grady clutched each other silently as

Ginger sang on. And eventually, first far away and then nearer and nearer they heard the slow, steady wing beat of the Awesome Bird.

Ginger's yodel grew quieter and quieter until it was almost a whisper. Puddles crept out from under the van.

The Awesome Bird swept over their heads.

"Keep singing!" urged Susan.

Ginger sang on.

The Awesome Bird flew backwards and forwards over the railway line. He circled the tops of the flats. He got in a tangle with the sycamore trees. And at long last, when Ginger was quite out of breath and Mrs O'Grady's mouth had fallen open so wide that if a fly had flown in she wouldn't have noticed, the Awesome Bird landed.

Now it is true that what was once a green between the flats and the railway line had shrunk to a grassy patch. And it is true that all the tall buildings of the city might have been distracting to a low-flying Awesome Bird. Whatever the reason the Awesome Bird didn't exactly land so much as flop, skid and spin and then – for want of dignity – spent fully five minutes huffing and puffing and fluffing its feathers, spreading out its wings for admiration and nudging Ginger with his beak.

Susan, blown over by the draught from the Bird's wings, lay on the ground looking, in her up-turned petticoats, much like a flower. Mrs O'Grady pulled her up and clutched close her kimono. Puddles' fur was blown every which way. Ginger, exhausted by his efforts, sat down on the steps of the van.

"Well," said Mrs O'Grady. "Not a very awesome landing."

"Sshhhh!" said Susan.

Once the Bird had recovered from his flight, they could see the whole grand height of him.

"You'll have to give me a leg up," said Mrs O'Grady. Ginger cupped his hands into a stirrup and Mrs O'Grady heaved herself up on to the back of the Bird.

With one clap of his wings, the Bird tossed her off.

"I think it has to be Ginger first," said Susan.

Obligingly the Bird knelt for Ginger. Dusting herself down and holding Puddles awkwardly in her arms, Mrs O'Grady climbed on next. Susan was last, her petticoats sticking out behind her like extra feathers.

The Awesome Bird had carried Rabobab children of all shapes and sizes but never before had he carried such a heavy load as Ginger, Mrs O'Grady, Puddles and Susan. He almost seemed to groan as he lifted off from land. Puddles' ears worked like extra propellers, his nose went into permanent quiver (as if even at this distance he was trying to sniff out Laurie) and never had his question mark of a tail been quite so questioning.

Ginger clutched the downy feathers at the Bird's neck. Mrs O'Grady clung on to Ginger with one arm and Puddles with the other. Susan put her arms round Mrs O'Grady's waist and hugged her tight.

"My, oh my!" was all Mrs O'Grady could say, over and over again. "My, oh my!"

But after a while, when the worst bumps of the flight were over, and they were high above the clouds, Mrs O'Grady grew more comfortable and chatty.

"Susan, can't you tell me *something* about the Rabo-bab?" she called over her shoulder.

"You know I can't," Susan shouted back. "And I dare say we shall find out soon enough."

"Just something like the colour of his socks," pleaded Mrs O'Grady. "Or what he has for breakfast."

"Really, Emily, there's something not quite serious

enough about you," said Susan. "Socks and breakfast indeed. The Rabobab is the Great Maestro of Light. And if
you *must* know, he doesn't wear socks and he eats sultanas
for breakfast. Now will you please be quiet, I want to
listen to the Song."

"I expect he has no-one to cook him bacon and eggs,"
said Mrs O'Grady.

Ginger, at the front, grinned.

"Sshhsh!" said Susan sharply, giving her friend more of
a squeeze than a hug.

So Mrs O'Grady shushed, and they flew on and on,
listening to the Awesome Bird's Song which lulled them
to sleep much as it had lulled Laurie.

And as Laurie's flight had taken all night, theirs took all
day, so that when at last they landed – or rather when at
last the Awesome Bird flumped down on the beach of
Rabobab Island and they all fell off in a heap – it was quite
dark.

Dark, that is, except for the beam from the Lighthouse
which swept the Island with light every night. The light
ran over them like bright fingers running through silk and
they all knew, knew at once, that this was special light,
newly-made light, pure light.

Ginger stood up and turned his face towards the light so
that when Mrs O'Grady next looked at him all the puzzle
and worry seemed to have gone out of his face.

Mrs O'Grady herself went through a long kind of wriggle as though the light tickled her through and through.
Puddles lay on his back and basked in it, waggling his legs
as if someone was stroking his tummy. As for Susan –
Susan just shone!

"Well," said Mrs O'Grady, trying not to smile. "Now
to find Laurie."

CHAPTER 13

Prisoners in Pink String

But at first they were almost too dazzled to find each other. Then, after much blinking, their eyes adjusted to the strange combination of love-light and moonlight. Mrs O'Grady looked about her. It had been impossible *not* to hope that Laurie would be there, waiting for her. Instead, what she saw made her gasp.

"Look!" said Mrs O'Grady pointing a shaking finger. Susan and Ginger looked. The beach, like a vast school dormitory, was covered in small woolly blue bags and in each bag was a child.

"What are they?" whispered Mrs O'Grady. (Giant, mother-eating blue snails, she was thinking.)

"Rabobab children," said Susan smiling even more. "They always sleep on the beach so the sea hushes them and the light washes them."

"Do you think my Laurie's among them?" asked Mrs O'Grady eagerly, but still whispering because it all felt so odd.

"No, he won't spend his first night here," said Susan. "He'll still be carrying too many memories to mix with the other children."

The mention of memories reminded Mrs O'Grady of

her worst fears, of Laurie forgetting her and Puddles, of losing all memory of home and wanting to stay on the Island for ever and ever. It brought back her courage and her temper. Mrs O'Grady was like all mothers when their children are in danger, tiger-fierce and fearless.

"I'm going to wake them up!" she announced.

"Oh don't!" pleaded Ginger. "They look like peas in pods."

Mrs O'Grady glared at him. "I'm not prepared to lose my Laurie just because they look like peas," she said. "The longer we dilly and dally, the more memories Laurie will lose, isn't that right, Susan?"

"I'm afraid so," Susan had to admit.

"Three days," said Mrs O'Grady, "before Laurie forgets his home altogether. And we've lost one day already, just getting here. We've two left. They'll have to be unpodded!" And with this Mrs O'Grady pulled tight the belt of her scarlet kimono and mounted a convenient rock. Susan, Puddles and Ginger tried to lurk behind her.

Mrs O'Grady was not used to making public speeches, let alone addressing strange blue-bagged children on an even stranger island. She began rather nervously.

"Is there anyone awake?" she called. A few bodies wriggled in a few blue bags.

Mrs O'Grady tried again.

"Ahoy there!" she called. "Is there anyone awake?"

A few sleepy heads appeared. One or two Rabobab children sat up rubbing their eyes and gazing in astonishment at the scarlet-robed figure on the rock.

Mrs O'Grady clapped her hands several times. Loudly. At that all the Rabobab children sat up. Some of them began wriggling out of their bags.

Now that she had their attention, Mrs O'Grady gained fresh courage.

"I am Laurie B. O'Grady's mother," she began.

At that all the Rabobab children scrambled out of their bags. They made a big semi-circle round her, although obviously they didn't dare come too close, and a loud whispering began.

"A mother, a mother, a mother," whispered the Rabobab children, passing the word to each other like a Chinese whisper.

"And this is Susan and this is Ginger and this is Puddles," continued Mrs O'Grady.

The Rabobab children didn't seem very interested in Susan or Ginger. Every Rabobab eye was fixed on Puddles and another round of whispering began.

"A Puddles!" murmured a tall boy to several smaller ones. "A Puddles!" And they all crept a little closer to look.

Puddles, delighted to be the centre of attention, used every friend-making trick he knew. He wagged his tail. He licked a great many small hands. He drooped his ears (usually a winner). He lay on his back and waved his paws in the air to indicate that those who wished to were welcome to tickle his tummy.

Eventually a very small child stretched out a hand and tried a tentative tickle. Puddles wriggled with delight. The Rabobab children laughed. Then they all wanted to pet and pat him. Puddles had never had such a fuss made of him.

"This is as mad as a circus," Mrs O'Grady said and she clapped her hands again.

The Rabobab children all ran backwards and fell silent.

"I have come here to look for my Laurie," said Mrs O'Grady. "My Laurie shouldn't be here . . ."

"Shouldn't be here . . ." echoed the Rabobab children

and their faces in the double light from the moon and the Lighthouse looked grave and alarmed.

"He was brought here by mistake," continued Mrs O'Grady, ignoring Susan who was tugging at her kimono. "The Awesome Bird made a mistake. He should have brought Ginger."

There was a sudden and complete silence. It was one of those awful silences that only happen when you have said something that never should be said. Mrs O'Grady almost lost her nerve. But she clasped her hands and thought hard of Laurie. Of Laurie losing his memory. Of Laurie liking it on the Island so much that he never wanted to come home. Of Laurie being what Susan called a 'Halvie' and of how much she wanted him to be a whole Laurie B. O'Grady, at home, in the world. Only two days left, Mrs O'Grady said to herself and bravely she ignored the silence and carried on saying what shouldn't be said.

"The Awesome Bird has made a mistake," she repeated. "Laurie has to come home and I have to find him. I have to see the Rabobab and tell him of the mistake. Now will you please tell me the way to the Rabobab."

Absolute silence.

Mrs O'Grady remembered war films she'd seen on television. She thought of army commanders. "You, you and you," she said, pointing her finger at the nearest Rabobab children. "Take me to the Rabobab."

But at that there was a kind of pandemonium. The Rabobab children gathered round them in a mob. Mrs O'Grady was pulled off the rock. Several children pulled out spools of pink string. Within minutes, Susan, Ginger and Mrs O'Grady were tied up in it. The child who had first tickled Puddles made a lead out of a piece of seaweed and tied Puddles to the end of it.

Mrs O'Grady, Susan and Ginger found themselves part of a long procession being pulled up the steep path by a gaggle of Rabobab children who were very soon singing.

"A Puddle, a muddle, befuddles us all,
A cuddle of Puddles deludeth us all,
All of a sudden a muddle of Puddles,
A huddle of cuddles befuddles us all."

"Where are they taking us?" Mrs O'Grady cried, wriggling in the pink string to call back to Susan.

"Now you've really got us in trouble," Susan replied. "If only you'd shown a little patience . . ."

"It's all very well for you," Mrs O'Grady shouted back. "You've got a continuous supply of children. All I've got is Laurie . . ."

"If you hadn't been so foolish as to say the Awesome Bird had made a mistake," said Susan, "we might not be tied up in pink string."

"But it's the truth!" protested Mrs O'Grady.

"Maybe," said Susan. "But there are some truths no-one wants to hear spoken out loud. And it's certainly not a truth the Rabobab wants to hear."

Up and up the steep cliff they climbed, moonlight showing them the way. Puddles was greatly enjoying himself. He felt like a pop star who has suddenly acquired a thousand new fans, for every now and again a different Rabobab child would hang back to pat him or stroke his ears or admire his wagging tail.

"Well, I'm not afraid of the truth," said Mrs O'Grady stoutly. "And I'm not afraid of the Rabobab."

But this was not entirely true.

The climb up the cliff was so long and so steep that Mrs O'Grady began to think the children might be taking them to the top simply to throw them off.

The night was beautifully warm and balmy and the beam from the Lighthouse and the dark gentle swish of the sea – now far below them – might have been soothing. But being tied up in string and pulled along by a gaggle of singing children was not. Besides, Mrs O'Grady, despite her show of bravery, was suffering from shock. The shock of the flight. The shock of the strange Island. The shock of Laurie vanishing in the middle of the night.

"Where are we going?" she kept asking. "Where are you taking us? Could you please untie me! I need to see the Rabobab. And where is my Laurie?"

The children ignored all these questions. They simply kept on singing. "A Puddle, a muddle, befuddles us all."

"We're going to the Lighthouse," said Ginger. (Ginger's Island memory was returning as Laurie's home memory was slipping away.)

Mrs O'Grady was very irritated by the way Ginger seemed to know things without anyone telling him.

"Why the Lighthouse?" she cried.

"Probably because the Lighthouse Keeper is the only one awake at this time of night," said Susan.

"And because they think we're intruders," said Ginger.

Mrs O'Grady saw that Ginger was right. The Lighthouse was exactly where they were going.

* * *

Fast asleep in the gentle swinging hammock of Janni Bean's sweet-smelling kitchen, Laurie dreamt of surfboarding on a huge slab of ginger cake.

CHAPTER 14

In the Dungeon

Little did Mrs O'Grady know, as she was tugged and hurried past the great domed Palace of Songs and Dreams, that she passed close by the sleeping Laurie.

The Lighthouse was only half a mile beyond. It stood on the edge of the cliff and close up, its beam was so bright that the whole procession had to duck and crawl under it.

A bell-rope hung outside the door but so high up that it took three Rabobab children, sitting on each other's shoulders, to pull it. Mrs O'Grady expected it to clang through the night like a great church bell, but it tinkled almost as quietly as her own front door bell. It was enough to startle the Lighthouse Keeper.

"Jupiter and Venus!" he grumbled. "Who in the planets wants to see me?" And he pressed the button that allowed the great arched door to creak slowly open.

"I don't like the look of this," said Mrs O'Grady, trying to resist the children tugging her in.

"I'll do my best to explain," said Ginger in an effort to comfort her.

"Sooner or later, they're sure to recognise Ginger," said Susan. "Though I'm afraid it won't be the Lighthouse Keeper who does so."

"Why ever not?" asked Mrs O'Grady.

"Because he's blind," said Susan.

But if Mrs O'Grady didn't like the look of the Lighthouse, Puddles liked it even less.

As the Rabobab children all tried to push through the door together – and got so stuck that some had to retreat while the first lot went through – Puddles broke free from the Rabobab children holding him and bolted.

"Puddles!" cried Mrs O'Grady, bursting into tears, "Puddles!"

Several Rabobab children ran after him, but Puddles, in full flight, was faster than any of them. He was as grey as the coming dawn – which helped – and he found himself a wonderful bush of rhododendrons and hid under it. Half a dozen Rabobab children dashed past without seeing him.

"First Laurie, now Puddles," wept Mrs O'Grady. "And it's all very well to say 'sooner or later' they'll recognise Ginger, but by then Laurie will have forgotten me completely."

"There's still time," said Susan squeezing Mrs O'Grady's hand as they were pushed up a long spiral staircase to the lamp room at the top of the Lighthouse.

It was almost dawn by the time they got there and the Lighthouse Keeper was rubbing his eyes and yawning for like an owl he slept by day and stayed awake all night. He sat in an enormous armchair before a range of dials and levers. The levers looked, to Mrs O'Grady, rather like the handles of beer pumps and there were labels above each of them, though of course the Lighthouse Keeper knew them by touch. The largest lever adjusted the beam of the great lantern.

The Lighthouse Keeper rose from his chair. He was a

small man with a great mass of wispy white hair and blind as he was, he had the brightest blue eyes Mrs O'Grady had ever seen. The sudden noise and confusion made wisps of his white hair stand on end.

The Lighthouse Keeper was a very solitary man. The only company he really enjoyed was his own and as he slept when everyone else was awake, days and months went by in which no-one visited him, neither the Rabobab children nor any of the other caretakers. Finnegan, on his rounds, was known to stop by and was usually welcomed as he never stayed long.

Although he was blind, the Lighthouse Keeper saw wonderful pictures in his mind because he was sent a continuous supply of dreams from the Palace. They were chosen by the Book-Keeper himself and sent by telepathy. The Lighthouse Keeper's mind was as open as the sea itself. Dreams floated in and out as easily as the waves. His days (asleep) were like a constant film show complete with the sound track of the songs.

He was looking forward to the latest dream – the new release, as you might call it – and much put out by what he considered a very bad-mannered interruption. He waved his arms in alarm at the number of voices and the scrabble of feet suddenly around him.

"Would someone tell me what is going on!" he demanded. "Why aren't you all asleep?"

"We've brought them," said the tallest Rabobab child.

"Brought who?" asked the Lighthouse Keeper.

"The invaders," said a chorus of voices.

"Invaders?" echoed the Lighthouse Keeper. For such a small man he had a very deep voice. It reminded Mrs O'Grady of the sea's boom on a stormy night.

In an effort to recover himself, the Lighthouse Keeper

pulled the lever that set the lantern on full beam despite the approaching dawn.

"You're all invaders!" he boomed. "What do you mean by disturbing me like this? Don't you know I've got work to do? The love-light level has to be exactly right. I expect you've thrown it right out of kelter now!"

Apart from a few whispers about muddles and puddles, the Rabobab children went very quiet.

"We found them on the beach," dared one.

"We captured them!" boasted a plump boy.

"We've got the one that calls herself a mother tied up in string," announced a small girl in very long shorts.

"We've got three of them and there was a Puddles," said a fourth child."

"But he escaped," said the littlest child mournfully.

"One at a time! One at a time!" boomed the Lighthouse Keeper. "A mother, did you say? And a Puddles?"

There was a chorus of 'yeses'.

"If you'd allow *me* . . ." began Mrs O'Grady.

The Lighthouse Keeper sank back in his enormous armchair. "A mother!" he said. "A voice from the Worldly World! Oh my lights and levers. How in the planets did she get here? And there are two more? And an alien called a Puddles."

The children all began talking at once again.

"Silence!" boomed the Lighthouse Keeper in a dangerously serious boom. "Why have you brought them to me? You know the Book-Keeper has the only Zap Line to the Rabobab?" And before the children could all begin again, the Lighthouse Keeper grabbed the child nearest to him. "You," he said. "Explain all this."

By chance, the Lighthouse Keeper had grabbed a particularly shy Rabobab child. "Well you see, sir," began the child, "we were all asleep, bathing under the light like we always do when . . ."

"Cut all that," said the Lighthouse Keeper, "and just tell me why you have brought them to me."

"The Book-Keeper's deep in stories all night," said the child. "He stories instead of sleeping. And besides you've got the dungeon . . ."

"Ah! The dungeon," said the Lighthouse Keeper thoughtfully. "I haven't been down there for years. Forgotten I had it."

"You've got the key too, sir," the child reminded him. "And we thought that would be the best place for the mother and others and the Puddle, only the Puddle escaped and . . ."

"That'll do!" said the Lighthouse Keeper who by now had had quite enough company for at least six months and was longing to be on his own again and begin his new dream. You could say that the Lighthouse Keeper was allergic to company and this was altogether far too much company.

The Lighthouse Keeper had two bunk beds in his lamp room. Sometimes he slept in the top bunk and sometimes he slept in the bottom. On the whole the top bunk seemed better for dreams. So now he began climbing the short ladder to the top bunk and plumping up his pillows.

"Speak to the Book-Keeper as soon as I wake up," he called down. "Intruders! His job. Not mine. The dungeon for now."

"Please sir, if we could just explain . . ." Susan called to the Lighthouse Keeper's disappearing legs.

". . . that you've got my Laurie!" cried Mrs O'Grady hearing the awful word 'dungeon'. "And I want him back!"

"And I belong here!" cried Ginger.

But at that moment the Lighthouse Keeper found the dungeon's huge key under his pillow and tossed it down to the shy Rabobab boy. All the children cheered and clapped. It was impossible for any of the three prisoners to make themselves heard in the hullabaloo.

The Lighthouse Keeper remembered something he had heard once in a dream and sat bolt upright in his bunk. "To the dungeon with them!" he boomed.

And with a great 'Hurrah!' the children pulled and pushed the three prisoners, down, down, down the spiral staircase, down below the big entrance door and into the dark, sea-damp dungeon. It took three of the strongest children to turn the huge key in the lock.

Up above, the Lighthouse Keeper flopped back in his bunk. "Peace and quiet!" said the Lighthouse Keeper. "Wonderful peace and quiet!"

At the edge of the horizon the sun was just beginning to rise like a great gold coin. The Lighthouse Keeper stretched and yawned, closed his eyes . . . and remembered he'd forgotten to turn off the light. Muttering and grumbling even more, he felt his way down the bunk's ladder and heaved up the lantern's lever to OFF. Then he climbed back into his bunk, closed his eyes and began emptying his mind so that the dream could begin.

"Tell the Book-Keeper later," he murmured to himself. "Intruders. His job. Not mine." And within minutes he was fast asleep.

Down in the dungeon Mrs O'Grady collapsed on a heap of old sacks. "*Now* what are we going to do?" she asked.

CHAPTER 15

♫

The Palace of Songs and Dreams

Janni Bean's method of waking Laurie was a simple one. She lowered the hammock and gently bumped him three times on the kitchen table.

It took Laurie a few minutes to realise that he wasn't in his own bed in Flat . . . Flat . . . But the number of the flat had somehow gone. Laurie climbed out of the hammock and slid off the table. The kitchen door was open and a crowd of Rabobab children were waiting outside, each with a breakfast bowl. They all seemed very excited about something.

"I tied them up!"

"No it was me!"

"Well I was the one who thought of the dungeon!"

Perhaps it was a game, thought Laurie, something like *Dungeons and Dragons*. Janni was so preoccupied with filling the breakfast bowls that she didn't seem to be listening. She made the children hush and form an orderly queue before ladling out a breakfast of what looked horribly like seaweed stew and a long finger of toast. Laurie saw the children disappearing into the cave houses laughing and chattering. He searched the queue for Gwen, but there was no sign of her.

When the last Rabobab child had run off, Janni turned to Laurie, tweaked a strand of his hair and said, "Umm. Still faded, I see. It had better be carrots."

Laurie gave a weak smile. There was not much to choose, he thought, between carrots and seaweed stew. Manfully he crunched his way through three carrots and was much relieved when Janni popped the big toaster and gave him several much marmaladed slices of toast. Janni kept studying his hair as if she expected it to change colour as she watched.

"Ginger cake?" she asked.

"Maybe later," said Laurie.

"Well, you'd better hurry along," said Janni. "I sent a message to the Book-Keeper that you were late arriving. But he'll be wanting your Memory Book."

"Oh yes. Yes, of course," said Laurie, almost choking on his last piece of toast.

"Maybe a few more carrots at lunch time will do it," said Janni and, as Laurie still lingered uncertainly, "Off you go then. I've jams to be making." And Janni turned to the pots and pans that she kept simmering and bubbling all through the night.

Slowly Laurie left the kitchen. Where *was* the Book-Keeper? And even if he found him, what was he to say? He was 'in the Book', Janni had said. But the truth, of course, was that Ginger, not Laurie, was in the book. And could he pretend that not only had he faded, but that he'd lost his red notebook – his Memory Book?

Laurie walked back down the long corridor. He could hear people in the music studios singing scales. On and on he walked, ever more slowly until he reached the entrance hall, and there, sitting on the bottom step of the stairs and grinning at him, was Gwen.

"Janni's fed you up, I can see," she said. Laurie was so pleased to see her that he grinned back.

"I thought you'd given up on me," he said.

Gwen looked quite offended. "Given up on you?" she said. "I slept here all night just so I wouldn't miss you this morning."

Laurie saw then that there were two rumpled rugs at the bottom of the stairs – Gwen's bed for the night.

"We made a pledge, remember?" said Gwen indignantly. "That we'd be friends and you'd stay forever."

"Yes," said Laurie. He felt ashamed of himself when he saw the rugs on the hard hall floor and thought of how he'd rocked gently to sleep in Janni's hammock. He wished he had another toffee for he didn't quite know how to say 'thank you'. He did what boys do and gave Gwen's arm a gentle punch. She seemed to understand this was a kind of thank you, for she smiled again and punched him back.

"You said that if I made up a splendid song, the Rabobab might summon me," said Laurie.

"And then you'd be a proper Rabobab child and not a Halvie," said Gwen.

"Yes," said Laurie a little uncomfortably, for it seemed that the two halves of him pulled in different directions so that he wanted *both* worlds, the Rabobab world and the Worldly World and that one without the other seemed no good at all. But he had more immediate problems to tackle.

"I think I'm already in trouble," he told Gwen. "Both Michael Finnegan and Janni have noticed that my hair isn't ginger. I told Janni my hair had faded."

Gwen giggled.

"It's not funny," said Laurie. "She's going to feed me

on nothing but marmalade, carrots and ginger cake until I'm gingerfied."

Gwen giggled some more.

"And now I've got to find the Book-Keeper," said Laurie.

"That's more serious," said Gwen. "You won't be able to kid him about fading. He keeps a record of all arrivals and departures. He has drawings too. Of all the caretakers, he's the one that knows each of us best. He has a full memory – that's why he's often so gloomy. But he'll know at once that you're not Ginger. Also, apart from the Awesome Bird, the Book-Keeper is the only one who has a regular audience with the Rabobab."

"So what are we to do?" asked Laurie. "What will happen to me? Will they send me back?"

"Oh no," said Gwen, looking quite shocked. "They wouldn't do that. I don't think anyone who had learnt the secrets of the Island would be allowed back."

"I can't say I have learnt any secrets yet," said Laurie. "I haven't learnt a single song or dream – or how to make either."

"You know about the Awesome Bird and the Sea of Forgetting," said Gwen. "That's quite enough to get you melted out altogether."

"Melted out!" cried Laurie. "What on earth – I mean, what on Rabobab Island do you mean?"

"I don't think it's ever actually *happened*," said Gwen. "But I think there's a rule somewhere in the Book-Keeper's books that says that anyone who arrives, uninvited by the Rabobab, will simply be melted. It would be the kindest thing to do."

"Kind?" cried Laurie. "Kind? To melt someone? To turn them into – into, well, nothing. It's a perfectly terrible thing to do!"

"No, no, no! You don't understand," said Gwen. "You wouldn't be turned into nothing. You'd be turned into love-light. It wouldn't hurt. In fact it would probably be rather nice – it's a gentle sort of sun-warming melt."

Laurie had a picture of himself as something rather like an ice-lolly dripping and melting in the sun.

"I do *not* want to be melted or turned into love-light," said Laurie determinedly. "However nice it is."

"We better think up a plan then," said Gwen.

"And fast," said Laurie.

"Well," said Gwen, looking rather coy. "As it happens, I am one of the Book-Keeper's favourites. So it's possible I could persuade him to help us."

"Do you mean he might talk to the Rabobab on my behalf?" asked Laurie eagerly. "Explain that it's not my fault that I'm here. That the Awesome Bird made a mistake."

Gwen sighed. "That's the snag," she said. "The Rabobab simply adores the Awesome Bird. He won't hear a word against him. We've all known that something's not quite right with the Awesome Bird for quite a while now. You're about the worst mistake he's made but . . ."

"Thanks!" said Laurie.

"But nobody has dared tell the Rabobab," finished Gwen.

"I could tell him myself!" cried Laurie (sounding much like his mother).

"You could," said Gwen. "Only it would probably mean Instant Melt."

"Oh," said Laurie, sinking down on the step beside Gwen and looking thoroughly dejected.

Gwen put an arm round him. "Don't worry," she said.

"The Book-Keeper is very clever. I'm sure he'll think of something."

The Book-Keeper's room was in the dome of the Palace. There were eight floors to the Palace and Laurie now saw that they had the choice of going up by the stairs or by a cable car that carried children up and down in much the way skiers are taken up and down mountains. The cable car looked great fun. Laurie thought how good it would be to have one in . . . where was it? In the flats, in Something Court – instead of the lift that didn't work. He imagined his mother coming home from work with a heavy bag of shopping, sitting herself in one of the little bucket seats and being hoisted up to the flat. The picture made him sad. Laurie pushed it from his mind. It suddenly seemed easier to wash time away than to suffer these small stabs of memory. And how much had he already forgotten in the Sea of Forgetting? Laurie didn't know.

Gwen saw Laurie look longingly at the cable car. "We could come down in it," she said. "If we walk up, I can show you all the studios and how the Dreamers and Songsters work and . . ."

"Oh yes!" said Laurie, cheering up at once for now, within the Palace, he felt close to something important, to something his heart had been telling him to do.

"And afterwards you can tell me about mothers," said Gwen firmly.

The Palace was the strangest building Laurie had ever been in – stranger than any ancient castle he had visited on school trips. As they went up the first flight of stairs, Laurie saw through the tall windows that the house was built round a large courtyard with a fountain in the centre. The dome was built across the four corners of the

Palace and its floor made a kind of awning across the courtyard, keeping it shady and cool.

More curiously the courtyard contained a great criss-cross of fine silver wires attached to the same slender poles Laurie had seen at the entrance to the Palace – only here the wires were all hung with notes, musical notes, silver notes, crotchets, quavers, minims, semi-quavers, all looking wet and drippy like so much washing hung on the line to dry. The 'washing', jingled and jangled and chimed very quietly.

"Some of the songs, drying," said Gwen as Laurie stopped to gaze out at the courtyard. "They'll go up to the Book-Keeper later. He'll transcribe them before they go out."

"Go out?" queried Laurie. "Go out where and how and who to?"

"To the Worldly World, of course," said Gwen. "The songs travel inside the dreams. You do *need* dreams down there, don't you?"

"Well, yes . . ." said Laurie.

"Finnegan says," said Gwen, "that without songs and dreams the hearts of the Worldly Ones would starve to death."

"I suppose that's true," said Laurie. "But exactly how do they travel?"

"The Rabobab sees to that," said Gwen. "Sometimes by laser beam, sometimes by air waves, sometimes by wind. The Rabobab has all kinds of mysterious ways."

Laurie was just about to ask another question about the Rabobab's mysterious ways when they reached the first floor of the Palace.

Gwen flung open the door of a long room full of Rabobab children. The walls were covered with pictures and strange lists of things that didn't seem to go together. Laurie saw a picture that looked like Buckingham Palace and another of what he thought was the Alps. The list nearest to him read 'teapot, County of Shropshire, kestrel, mackerel sky, spaghetti, daisies in May'.

"This is the pool," said Gwen.

Laurie looked around for some kind of swimming pool and then realised that it was not that kind of pool. This was where all kinds of Worldly information was 'pooled' or gathered. And as if to confirm this, he saw dozens of small red notebooks – exactly like Ginger's.

"I'm off duty today," said Gwen. "But I often work in here."

"Don't you make songs and dreams?" asked Laurie, rather disappointed.

"I'm still a music apprentice," said Gwen. "I'm learning about all different sounds and rhythms. And besides, I won't graduate until I've visited."

"Visited?"

"The Worldly World," said Gwen. "I haven't had my time down There. With a mother," she added wistfully.

"What do they do with all these lists and pictures and notebooks?"

"They're the ingredients for the songs and dreams," said Gwen. "You see to make something new you have to take something already existing, or lots of already existing old things, and mix them together until you get something new. Come on, I'll show you the studios."

Up on the next floor were dozens of small rooms and from each came the sound of a different voice or instrument. There was someone singing a rather odd pop song. Another voice singing a rapp. A third, a blues. There were merry violins and very sad cellos and someone on drums and when Laurie looked through the window into the courtyard he saw fresh notes streaming out on to the silver wires.

"Would you like to meet a Songster?" asked Gwen.

"Yes please!" said Laurie.

Gwen knocked politely on a studio door. The singing stopped and the Songster opened the door. She was a tall, slender girl with pale, wispy hair tied up in a hasty pony-tail.

"This is Meryl," said Gwen and, to avoid naming Laurie, she added hurriedly, "We're on our way to the Book-Keeper."

"You must have done your visit," said Meryl.

"Well – yes, I suppose I have," said Laurie. (It had been a rather long visit, he thought to himself. All of eleven years.)

Meryl picked up a piece of paper, her song ingredients sent up from the pool. "The trouble with songs," said Meryl, "is that they do have to stick in people's minds even after the dream has faded. At least they do if they're to be of any use."

"Exactly what sort of use do you mean?" asked Laurie as politely as he could, for he had never really thought of songs as *useful*. Behind him he could hear Gwen sighing.

"Well," said Meryl. "This song is to go with a dream that's to inspire a painting, so somehow it's got to be full of colours and shapes. Last week I had to make one that would inspire a totally new pudding, a pudding no-one had ever tasted before. So that had to be full of mouth watering sounds. I made a song frothy as sea foam. I was quite pleased with it. But this one is really difficult."

Laurie saw that all kinds of notes dangled from the ceiling in various groups and sizes. Meryl had a frame about the size of a large painting, strung with even finer silver wires than those that ran across the courtyard.

Laurie watched as she pulled down four semi-quavers and a minim, hung them on her frame and then tried singing them.

"Not quite right," she said, "but nearer. I'm afraid I can't stop now. If I stop in mid-song, I'll have to begin all over again. Come and see me another time."

Laurie and Gwen left Meryl to her song. There were studios on the next three floors. As they climbed up to the fifth floor the cable car went past them with several Rabobab children swinging in the bucket seats. It was still early morning and the children only just getting to work.

The Dream-Makers' studios began on the fifth floor and were quite different from those of the Songsters. They were larger and all in darkness and each room had an enormous screen in it. The Rabobab children worked in groups on the dreams.

"They won't notice if we sneak in," said Gwen.

It was like going into a rather strange cinema, only there was no projector. The Rabobab children seemed to beam images from their eyes, so that as Laurie watched he saw a dream that included mermaids with an under-water computer, a castle next door to a supermarket and a man growing wings.

"How do they do it?" Laurie whispered to Gwen as each child added a new image to the dream. "It's like painting without a paintbrush or writing without a pen."

"Direct Imagination," Gwen whispered back. "They're not weighted with sorrow, like your Worldly Ones and then they've bathed in the love-light for years and years. But they couldn't do it without the information coming back from the Visits. And they couldn't do it if the Worldly Ones didn't respond. If a song or a dream is ignored it has a terrible effect on the Island."

"Like what?" whispered Laurie.

"We *must* get to the Book-Keeper," said Gwen. "I'll tell you on the way."

They crept out of the Dream Studio.

"When the dreams and songs are ignored," said Gwen as they began climbing towards the dome, "the love-light starts to grow weaker and weaker. It's a two way process you see. The Rabobab collects the light and then . . ."

"Wait . . . wait," cried Laurie. "What do you mean, the Rabobab collects the light?"

Gwen stopped halfway up the stairs. "Don't you even know that?" she asked. "That's what the Rabobab is about. Light. Collecting light. Turning it into love. Love-light. That's all he cares about. Well, light and the Awesome Bird."

"I see," said Laurie. "And what about all the children? What about us down there? Doesn't he care for people?"

"He hasn't time for people in *particular*," said Gwen scornfully. "Can't you imagine how hard it is turning light into love? That takes the Maestro all his time and energy. And then all that love sent down in songs and dreams has to be reflected back to us. That makes the light stronger. And it keeps the love-level constant. If that doesn't happen – well, instead of love, there's just a sort of murk."

They had reached the dome now. It reminded Laurie of a huge, circular library and indeed above two big doors was the word 'Book-Room'. It was the only sign Laurie had seen anywhere on the Island.

"Here we are," said Gwen. "Tidy yourself up a bit, can't you?"

Laurie pulled down his T-shirt and smoothed his hair. He wished he wasn't wearing slippers. Suddenly he felt very nervous.

"Do you think the Book-Keeper will help me?" he asked.

"He's the only one that can," said Gwen.

CHAPTER 16

A Damp Dungeon and
a Jammy Kitchen

The dungeon was dark, damp and noisy. The noise was the sea crashing against the rocks beneath the Lighthouse and echoing upwards. They almost had to shout to make themselves heard and after a while the sound of the sea seemed to be inside their own heads.

The only light came through an iron grille set high in the wall which sent a bar of gold sunshine slanting down towards the dismal group sitting on the floor.

Mrs O'Grady had made a kind of cushion of sacks. Susan and Ginger had found an old box each. They sat round the slant of sunshine as if they were sitting round a fire.

"Well, at least we won't be short of food," shouted Susan. "It looks as if they use this place as a kind of larder."

And when they looked more closely into the gloomy corners of the dungeon, Mrs O'Grady and Ginger saw that this was true. The dungeon was lined with shelves. There were tins of biscuits, boxes of dried apricots, pots of nuts and bottles labelled *Fizz*, *Whizz* and *Pop*.

"I've lost my appetite," bawled Mrs O'Grady. "I've lost my son, my dog and my appetite. And I think I'm beginning to lose heart."

104

The dungeon seemed to sharpen Ginger's appetite. He set to on biscuits, dried apricots and a bottle of *Whizz*.

"A fine pickle we're in now," shouted Mrs O'Grady, watching Ginger eat. "And I trusted you two. Why haven't they recognised Ginger as one of their own? And why can't Ginger do something?"

"He hasn't been in the sea, that's why," said Susan. "He's still got the smell of the Worldly World on him. Like we have. And it's no good blaming us, Emily. If you hadn't decided to wake up all the children and demand to see the Rabobab things might be very different."

"And no Puddles," said Mrs O'Grady loudly but mournfully. "Really, things couldn't be worse."

"That might, just might be a good thing," Susan shouted back, helping herself to a biscuit from the tin Ginger was demolishing at great speed.

"Poor Puddles, lost and alone on a strange island without me or Laurie to look after him. What can be good about that?" asked Mrs O'Grady.

"Puddles might just find Laurie," Ginger yelled through a mouthful of biscuits.

"Of course!" said Mrs O'Grady smiling for the first time that day. Hope and her appetite came back together. She began on a pot of nuts. "Puddles will find Laurie," she shouted over a particularly large crash of waves, "and Laurie will find us and then we'll go and find this wretched Rabobab!"

"It won't be as simple as that," shouted Susan, trying to be brief because shouting seemed to take up a lot of energy. "The Island's large. Not easy for Puddles. The Book-Keeper is our other hope."

"The Book-Keeper?" queried Mrs O'Grady.

"He has the Zap line to the Rabobab," Ginger reminded her. "And the Lighthouse Keeper is meant to tell him that we're here."

"As invaders," said Mrs O'Grady. Her hopes went up and down like the waves themselves.

"Yes," said Susan. "But I know the Book-Keeper of old. I think he'll remember Ginger. He's the only one here, apart from the Rabobab himself – and *do* speak of him with a little more respect Emily – who has a proper memory. The problem is, will the Lighthouse Keeper remember to tell the Book-Keeper about us?" This speech exhausted Susan. She helped herself to a bottle of *Fizz*.

"How can he possibly forget?" shouted Mrs O'Grady.

"Unfortunately, quite easily," croaked Susan.

* * *

Michael Finnegan's rounds of the Island included regular visits to Janni Bean's kitchen.

"Just need a little something to keep me going," he would say, sitting himself down at Janni's table, and she would butter him a fresh crust of bread, topping it with one of her new and experimental jams, or present him with a small white dish of dark red shiny cherries.

He arrived that morning soon after breakfast. Janni gave him a mug of frothy iced coffee. (It was known as 'Finnegan's Favourite' on the Island because it was very cooling after a hot donkey ride.)

Janni, who rarely sat down (except at Snooze Time, when she slept in the hammock), waited until he'd finished his coffee and wiped the froth from his mouth. She could tell he was troubled.

"That child who's just come back," began Finnegan, giving his whiskers a quick tug before they went in again.

"Ginger, you mean?" said Janni Bean.

"A very ungingery Ginger," said Finnegan.

"He seems to have a bad case of memory lag," said Janni. "And his hair has certainly faded. Plenty of sleep and swimming and a proper diet and he'll soon recover."

"Umm!" said Finnegan. "I'm not so sure. In my opinion I don't think he's Ginger at all. I don't think he's a proper Rabobab child."

"Oh my jams and jellies!" exclaimed Janni. "Who is he then and how has he got here?"

"I think," said Finnegan carefully, "he's what they call a Halvie – a few have been known over aeons of time – children who belong to both Here and There or There and Here, depending on how you look at it. As for how he got here . . . well, I'm afraid . . . well, the Awesome Bird has been behaving very oddly recently."

"You don't think . . . ?" said Janni. (A pan on the stove bubbled over. Janni hastened to rescue it.)

"That AB has brought the wrong child?" said Finnegan. "I'm afraid I do."

"He's made mistakes before," said Janni, offering Finnegan a saucer of newly set jam to dip his finger in, "Arriving in the wrong place, or being too late or too early, but nothing as serious as this. In my opinion he's just become too puffed up for his own good. He's the Rabobab's darling. He thinks he can do no wrong."

"I'm not so sure," said Finnegan. "I think he might be poorly."

"Nonsense!" said Janni briskly. "He's just grown vain and idle. And what are we going to do about it? There's a Rabobab child abandoned down There and the wrong child Here. *Someone's* got to tell the Rabobab."

The two of them looked at each other.

"Well," said Finnegan uneasily, "the Songsters and Dreamers must have noticed by now . . ."

"Oh they'll have noticed all right," said Janni. "But will they dare do anything?"

"I have my rounds," said Finnegan evasively.

"And I can't possibly leave my pans on the boil," said Janni.

"Perhaps," said Finnegan, after another long silence, "I could go and see the Awesome Bird . . . while I'm on my rounds."

"Give him a good talking to," said Janni.

"Well, inquire into his health," said Finnegan nervously. "The Rabobab would certainly want to know if AB wasn't well."

"That's true," said Janni. "Though my guess is that you'll find AB is very well indeed and simply trying to cause trouble. Attention seeking – as if he doesn't get enough of that as it is."

"Only from the Rabobab," said Finnegan.

Janni looked quite shocked. "Well, isn't that enough for anyone?" she asked.

"I don't know," said Finnegan. "Speaking for myself, I like lots of attention from lots of people."

"Well," said Janni, "when will you visit?"

"Perhaps at Snooze Time," said Finnegan. "I'll come and tell you what I find out."

* * *

Behind the rhododendron bush, Puddles was snoozing already. When he woke up he felt – as Mrs O'Grady had imagined he would feel – both lost and lonely.

But Puddles had sound instincts and an even sounder nose. Puddles began to explore.

CHAPTER 17

One Chance

At first Laurie could hardly see the Book-Keeper for books. There were shelves and shelves and shelves of them going all round the dome and stretching up to the ceiling. There were dream records and song records in alphabetical order. There were a great many large atlases and fat encyclopaedias. There was an enormous bookcase labelled 'Diaries from Down There' which seemed full of red notebooks of various sizes. There were tall gold-edged volumes labelled *Songs* and big flat round tins (like film reels) labelled *Dreams* (for the Book-Keeper kept copies of all the songs and dreams). There was one shelf with a line of cloth-bound books each entitled *Rabobab Register* and a similar line of *Annals of the Island* and, on the Book-Keeper's desk, two big baskets labelled *Children Here* and *Children There*.

As Gwen shut the door behind them, Laurie saw that the Book-Keeper was perched at the top of a ladder fetching down a large dusty volume.

"My dear Gwen," said the Book-Keeper. "How very pleasant to see you! How very pleasant indeed!" And he came nimbly down his ladder on his long, elegant legs. "I was wondering when you'd call. I'm much in need of dusting down."

As if she was quite used to this, Gwen picked up a clothes brush from the desk and climbed on a chair. The Book-Keeper turned himself round and round so that she could brush off the dust. When she had done so, and when the Book-Keeper had given himself an extra shake, Laurie saw that he was a tall man with a great deal of curly grey hair and three pairs of spectacles balanced on his nose. He had a permanent stoop from much bending over many books.

The Book-Keeper removed two pairs of spectacles to peer carefully at Laurie and then putting one hand on top of Laurie's head, twizzled him round like a spinning top.

"Oh dear, oh dear, oh dear," said the Book-Keeper. "A Halvie! Well I never! That Awesome Bird has really done it this time!" And he reached for the Zap Line to the Rabobab.

"Stop!" cried Gwen. "This is Laurie and he's my very best pledged friend! We want you to help us!"

The Book-Keeper put down the scarlet Zap phone (it had but a single 'R' button on the front) and put on his extra spectacles.

"But Gwen, dear," he said, "I'm really not sure I can. And you know it's my duty to inform the Rabobab . . ."

"I know," said Gwen, "But if you could just wait . . . if you could give Laurie a chance. He wants to stay here forever and become a proper Rabobab child."

The Book-Keeper turned to Laurie. "Are you sure about that?" he asked.

Now the truth is that Laurie wasn't at all sure. On the beach with Gwen, and then swimming in the sea, he had felt as sure as sure as sure. And a buzz of excitement had run through him when he had seen the Song- and Dream-Makers at work. It was as if he had found another family, people who – in some odd kind of way which Laurie couldn't explain to himself – he belonged to . . . and yet . . . and yet . . . as the Book-Keeper regarded him gravely and patiently, he didn't feel sure. Not *wholly* sure. Only – well – *half* sure.

For no reason whatsoever he thought of Puddles bounding through the park. He thought of his own bedroom and being snugged up under his duvet. He thought of his mother's cottage pie. All these memories, that hadn't yet been washed away, flashed through his mind and heart as the Book-Keeper waited.

And then Laurie looked at Gwen. Her seaweedy hair was all over the place. Her eyes were fixed on him with absolute trust. He had promised her. They had pledged.

"Yes, I'm sure," said Laurie.

Gwen hopped up and down with excitement.

"We thought if Laurie could prove himself," she said. "If he could compose a song and sing it to the Rabobab, then the Rabobab would allow him to stay. He'd make him a full-time Rabobab child."

"But what about the child who *should* have come back?" asked the Book-Keeper. He riffled through the papers in his *Children There* basket. "Ginger," he said. "He's the boy Awesome Bird should have brought back."

"Ginger likes it down there," said Laurie. "He told me so himself. He thought I was very lucky." Laurie got a sudden lump in his throat thinking of Ginger down in the van, Ginger perhaps walking Puddles or Ginger and Susan having tea with his mother.

"Umm," said the Book-Keeper, moving his spectacles up and down his nose, "I doubt that feeling will last for Ginger. He's sure to get homesick soon enough. You'll know something about that feeling, I expect," he added, putting a comforting arm round Laurie's shoulders, "though the Sea of Forgetting will wash it away . . ."

"So you *will* help?" begged Gwen. "Please, please, *please!*"

No-one, thought Laurie, could resist Gwen's 'pleases' which came accompanied by a very large smile and a jiggle and joggle of her seaweedy curls.

"It will mean a tough session in the Song Studios," said the Book-Keeper. "Laurie will find it very hard and success can't be assured . . ."

Laurie and Gwen both jumped up and down at this.

"I'll work terribly hard," said Laurie. "When do I begin?"

"You better do a bit more swimming first," said the Book-Keeper. "There's still a lot of times past sticking to you. And I need to fix things up with the Studios. Come back here at teatime. We may have to work through the night. And I have to tell you this – I can only give you one chance."

"I'll only need one," said Laurie, for now he was so excited about working in the Song Studios that all thought of home vanished from his mind.

"Off you go then," said the Book-Keeper. "And here's something you better be thinking about." He scribbled something on a piece of paper and gave it to Laurie.

Laurie read it as he and Gwen, each perched in a bucket seat of the cable car, swung down, down, down to the entrance hall of the Palace of Songs and Dreams.

What the Book-Keeper had written was this:

> 'A watched song
> Never sings.'

* * *

It took Michael Finnegan a long time to reach the nest of the Awesome Bird. The Bird lived in the tallest eucalyptus tree in the far north of the Island.

The branches of the tree were hung with Orders from the Rabobab written on coloured twists of paper and scraps of discarded songs and dreams. Each Rabobab Order had a long tag or tail attached to it.

It was well into Snooze Time when Finnegan arrived. To let Awesome Bird know he was there, he sang a few rounds of his song. There was an angry rustling from up above and a few Orders fell at Finnegan's feet. Finnegan picked up a couple. The tag on the first read 'Collect Harry from Sheffield, Tuesday night'. The tag on the second read 'Deliver Polly to S. at dawn on Friday'. It was impossible to tell how old or new were the Orders from the Rabobab. Had Harry been collected? Polly delivered? Finnegan didn't know.

As he read on, there was more angry rustling from above and a further shower of Orders and song scraps, like tiny folded kites, fell about him. It seemed as if the Awesome Bird's nest was rather like a waste-paper basket full of neglected messages.

Finnegan tethered his donkey, climbed half way up the tree, settled himself on a convenient branch from which he could just about see the Bird and called up to him.

"I say, old chap," he said. "You seem in a bit of a mess!"

For answer the Bird used his legs to kick out another batch of scraps and Orders, then he flumped down inside his nest, turned his back on Finnegan and closed his eyes.

"I see how it is," said Finnegan. "You're overworked and unhappy."

No answer.

Finnegan gave a scratch to his whiskers during their brief appearance and tried to put some of the Orders back on the branches. "The thing is," he continued, "we've got a bit of a problem."

There was something between a squeak and a squawk from Awesome Bird. Finnegan couldn't tell if it was a sad or an offended squeak-squawk.

"You probably know about it really," he said, as tactfully as he could. "Somehow or another, we have the wrong child on the Island. We *should* have a Ginger, but I think we've got a Halvie. Of course everyone makes a mistake now and again . . . " he added.

The Awesome Bird buried his head deep into his feathers.

Finnegan waited a while. "I was going to suggest," he said. "That if you could quietly do a quick flight and a swop – take the Ungingery one back to There and bring the Gingery one Here – well then, we could let bygones be bygones and the Rabobab need never know."

This time Awesome Bird gave a sound that was a cross between a snore and a snort, fluffed and huffed his feathers, threw out a few more song scraps and curled himself into a feathery puff ball.

"I see how it is," said Finnegan. "You are a very despairing Bird. Possibly with heart-ache."

The Bird snuffled a little.

"Well," said Finnegan, stretching his legs which had grown rather cramped. "I'll do my best for you old chap. I'll try to explain to the Rabobab that you are not feeling at all well – he'll have to know, of course – and I'll remind him of your True Awesomeness."

There was total silence from above.

With a sigh Finnegan climbed down the tree, hung up an Order or two and mounted his donkey.

"I'll take a roundabout approach," he called up. "I always think people understand that best. Though," he added to himself as he rode away, "you never can tell *what* the Rabobab will understand and what he won't."

CHAPTER 18

♫

A Roundabout Way
to the Rabobab

Up in the mountains, in his tower of many turrets, the Rabobab tended his candles and lamps, stirred his great vats of light, fluttered in a few pink oleander petals, crushed in a pestle of crimson geraniums, added several ladles of oil, a drop or six of wine, six leaves of clover, a handful of raisins and sultanas and then he whisked everything together, whistling as he did so.

Set in the ground, all round the Rabobab's residence, were great wells of collected light that had to be checked, daily, for purity. They shone so brightly even the Rabobab had to wear sunglasses to look at them.

The Rabobab was Very Everything. Very Whiskered, Very Old, Very Small and Very Energetic. He did not so much walk as hop, sometimes on one leg, sometimes on the other.

Apart from Awesome Bird, who had a regular audience with him, nobody saw much of the Rabobab and indeed nobody much wanted to. A white flag flew from the topmost turret of the Rabobab's tower with the letters OO written on it. This meant Otherwise Occupied. Only very occasionally, about once every six years, did the Rabobab fly a blue flag with VB on it (Very Bored) which meant that he would be glad of visitors.

What the Rabobab was Very Occupied with was love
and the making of it. And very hard work it was too.
What mattered to the Rabobab was keeping the love-level
down There steady – in a constant flow, you might say, as
of electricity, or water. It should have been easy. Love
went into all the dreams. It was the chief ingredient. Only
love could give a dream, oomph, vitality, spark. Only love
could make a dream vivid and alive. Without it a dream
was like a poor television film no-one would watch.

The Rabobab used love of all kinds and varieties.
Love-of-a-child, love-of-a-garden, love-that-was-a-new-
medicine, love-as-singing-your-heart-out, love-as-mending-
an-old-fence, love-as-planting-a-tree and, of course, the
more common falling-in-love kind of love.

This last was a particular source of difficulty to the
Rabobab, for the Worldly Ones down There would fall in
and out of it with amazing speed, or love the wrong person, or love too much or too little. They were an Unsteady
Lot down There, there was no doubt about it, and all this
unsteadiness affected the love-level.

In addition to this, there were times when the Worldly
Ones seemed resistant to love. Their receivers (as the
Rabobab called their hearts) didn't seem to be working
properly. Dazzling dreams, daring dreams, the sweetest
of dreams could be sent off to them by beam, by wave,
by wind and they sort of bounced off their skins. The
Worldly Ones didn't want to know. They didn't want to
listen. In some way or another they had shut down their
receivers. Sometimes it was temporary. Sometimes it
was long-lasting. (When it was long-lasting, the Rabobab
put up a grey flag with VFU on it – meaning Very Fed
Up.)

When the Worldly Ones didn't want to know, the

Rabobab's work became very hard, almost impossible. Unless the Wordly Ones responded to dreams – let them into the atmosphere, so to speak – no light was reflected back to the Island. The two-way system broke down. The light grew paler and weaker. There was the danger of the Island clouding over. It is difficult to understand, but the Rabobab did not care Who Loved Who, or Who Loved What or How. The making of love itself, out of the light collected in the wells, was a full time job – more than a job, an obsession. At night the light the Rabobab turned into love was pumped underground through pipes (like water pipes) up to the Lighthouse. This was the love-light that nightly washed over the children who slept on the beach so that they were properly fed with love. (The cave houses, beautifully cool at Snooze Time in the mid-day heat, were too hot at night.)

But apart from his preoccupation with the love-level, there was one special love in the Rabobab's own life, and that was his love for his messenger, the Awesome Bird.

More ages ago than even the Rabobab could remember, a Rabobab child woke from the night's light-washing, having dreamt an Awesome Bird. And having dreamt him, she sang him, and having sang him, he appeared – flying slowly in over the sea and the mountains and landing softly and gently in a flurry of perfectly white feathers on a turret of the Rabobab's tower. And although the Rabobab had given the child both the light and the dream, he had not imagined such a perfect, such a beautiful creature as this.

"My Awesome Bird!" he said, so that the Bird flew down from the turret to the Rabobab's feet. In those days, the beauty of the Bird was such that the Rabobab wept. He knew instantly that the advent of the Bird could make an enormous difference both to life on the Island and life down There.

The Rabobab saw at once the possibility of sending the children on visits down There and how useful this could be in making accurate songs and dreams. Songs and dreams that the Worldly Ones could understand. (The Rabobab was Very Hot on accuracy.) A child who had lived down There would learn to understand how the receivers of the Worldly One worked, and, as a result, would be able to make dreams that really moved them.

And so Awesome Bird was given the grandest tree on the Island for his nest, breakfasts of honeyed nuts and regular meetings with the Rabobab. The two of them would sit together in silent happiness, the Rabobab in a rather elegant purple and gold deck chair on his balcony and Awesome Bird perched on a nearby turret. The Rabobab would tell Awesome Bird again and again how beautiful he was, what a fine and awesome bird. And Awesome Bird would preen and fluff his feathers and eventually, lulled by the affection in the Rabobab's voice, would sleep. It was a special sort of loving sleep.

So dearly did the Rabobab favour Awesome Bird, that the Bird could do no wrong and in the eyes of the Rabobab, Awesome Bird remained as perfect as on the day he had arrived. Everyone on the Island knew this. And so, although in the Palace of Songs and Dreams there were certain rumours going about, that all was not well with Awesome Bird and that, when seen, there was a certain sulky look about him, no-one dared say so to the Rabobab.

Only Michael Finnegan, Janni Bean, the Lighthouse Keeper and now the Book-Keeper, knew that the Awesome Bird had brought the wrong child to the Island. And only Finnegan knew just how bad things were with Awesome Bird.

The Songsters and Dreamers told each other that the Bird was just going through a bad patch. He would be awesome again, soon enough. Besides, no-one had failed to notice that the Otherwise Occupied flag had been flying fairly continuously from the Rabobab's tower and that when this was so, it meant that the Rabobab was working in a frenzy of almost wild concentration. To visit him at such a time might well be to risk being tipped into one of the wells and melted into extra love-light, an act which the Rabobab seemed to believe was a kindness, although no-one else quite agreed with him.

Michael Finnegan thought of all this as he made his slow, roundabout, clip-clopping way up to the Rabobab's tower.

* * *

For the Lighthouse Keeper, Snooze Time lasted all day. But that day – Laurie's second on the Island – the Lighthouse Keeper's sleep was a troubled one. He knew there was *something* he should remember, but he just couldn't quite think what it was. He kept waking up to the question 'What was it? What was it?' and falling asleep again.

Sometimes a little of the Rabobab children's chant slipped into his dream so that he sang to himself 'A Puddle, a muddle, deludeth us all'. But it didn't help him to remember *why* the children had come or what they were singing about so that at last he gave up on it, pulled the blankets firmly over his head, recited the number of jams made by Janni,

> raspberry
> apricot
> bramble
> quince
>
> gooseberry
> pomegranate
> lichee
> plum
>
> loganberry
> mango
> cherry
> peach

and then he was fast asleep.

Down in the dungeon, Mrs O'Grady, Susan and Ginger could tell the day was passing by the bar of sunshine coming through the grille – so hot and brightly sharp at mid-day that it was like the blade of a sabre, and gradually softening and filling with dust motes as the afternoon wore on. And what a long day it seemed!

Now and again, a curious Rabobab child, perched on the shoulders of another, would peer through the grille at them, giggle and vanish before any of them could call out.

"He's forgotten us, hasn't he?" said Mrs O'Grady mournfully. "The Lighthouse Keeper. He's forgotten us entirely. And by now I expect Laurie has forgotten us too. It's his second day. I expect more than half his memory has been washed away."

"Don't give up hope," said Susan. "There's still Puddles."

"The sea washes time away, but not love," said Ginger. "I've just remembered that. And that means Laurie won't forget you in his heart."

"But I want him in my arms!" cried Mrs O'Grady.

"Give Puddles a chance," urged Susan. "Animals are often wiser than we are."

"Puddles," said Mrs O'Grady, "is very loving, very loyal and often very silly."

"Well, that sounds very hopeful to me," said Susan firmly. "Pass the biscuits, Ginger. There's still time either for someone to rescue us or for us to find a way out of here."

"Still time," repeated Mrs O'Grady gloomily. "But not much of it."

★ ★ ★

All afternoon, while Mrs O'Grady, Ginger and Susan languished in their dungeon, while the Lighthouse Keeper slept forgetfully on and while Puddles – who, by this time, had had a sniff of Laurie – was searching the Island for him, Laurie and Gwen played on the beach and swam in the sea.

And as Laurie soon discovered, there is no greater or more gorgeous delight than swimming in the Sea of Forgetting. To swim in those waters was like swimming in the sky. Indeed the sea and sky so melted into one another that it was like being within a vast and airy bubble of blue.

Then there was the crystal sparkle of this sea that made Laurie's skin tingle and the waves – such waves! They bounced you and rolled you. They lifted you up and slid you off their backs. They were for falling into like a great blue duvet. They rushed up to you, those waves, and took you into a big watery hug. And they washed and washed away all memory of sorrow, until, Laurie felt, he was almost as new as a new day.

It was true, as Michael Finnegan had said, that the Sea of Forgetting washed away time but not love, so that Laurie didn't forget his mother, Susan, Ginger and Puddles. They were there, in his heart, but he felt no great need to see them or to think about them.

In any case, with Gwen around still pestering him with questions about mothers, it wouldn't have been possible for him to forget his own.

"Tell me what your mother is like?" said Gwen when, between swims, they lay flopped on the beach.

"Well," said Laurie (finding that he had to work quite hard to remember), "she's sort of rounded and tubby."

"Like Michael Finnegan?" asked Gwen.

"No," said Laurie. "Finnegan is big and round and prickly. My mother is small and round and cuddly."

"Oh," said Gwen in a very small voice. "And does she cuddle you lots?"

"Oh yes!" said Laurie not noticing the small voice. "Lots and lots and lots. There's a hug when I get up in the morning and a hug and cuddle when I come home from school and a big one when I go to bed."

"And kisses?" asked the same small voice.

Laurie didn't like to admit to too many kisses. "Just a few," he said carelessly.

"How many a day?" persisted the same small voice.

"Er – er – well, perhaps a dozen," said Laurie.

"Twelve whole kisses a day?" cried Gwen and burst into tears.

Laurie put an arm round her. "Don't worry," he said. "Your turn will come for going down There, and then you'll have a mother. For a time at least. You might even get Susan."

And then he had to start all over again and tell her about Susan and the van with the octopuses on it and the little gas stove and Susan's petticoats and the way she danced and sang and cooked lovely fat sausages and certainly gave you lots of hugs, kisses and cuddles. (By the next morning Laurie would have forgotten all these things.)

"I hope I *do* get Susan," said Gwen, when he'd finished.

"If you get Susan, you'll have a share of my mother too," said Laurie. And that thought made him feel so very odd that he had to go swimming again.

"You'd better go off to the Book-Keeper now," said Gwen when they had had a final wave-jumping, sea-tumble. "He'll be expecting you. I'll meet you here tomorrow morning. By then you'll have made your song. Good luck!"

"Thanks," said Laurie. "I've tried not to think about the song because of the Book-Keeper's note. 'A watched song never sings'."

"He's right," said Gwen. "A song has to grow in your heart."

"I hope it has," said Laurie nervously.

"I hope so too," said Gwen. "Pledge?"

"Pledge!" answered Laurie and they both slapped hands.

Gwen watched as Laurie slowly began climbing up the path to the Palace of Songs and Dreams.

The sun was sinking into the sea. Slowly the sky blushed red.

* * *

All day Puddles had searched and searched for Laurie. He had kept himself hidden, peering into the cave houses only during Snooze Time. He had been on the beach in the morning, when all the children were at work in the Palace and in the afternoon he had wandered up the remote mountain paths near – although he didn't know it – the Rabobab's tower. And although two or three times he thought he had caught the scent of Laurie, now he had lost it.

Puddles was hungry and exhausted. The very pads of his paws felt quite worn out. He found himself a bed of bouncy basil and slept.

CHAPTER 19

Finnegan Fails

From the height of his tower the Rabobab saw Finnegan approaching from a great distance and he was not pleased. He tossed a few ladles of light over the side of one turret and they splashed like liquid rainbows on the ground below.

Finnegan clip-clopped on and, although he could plainly see the Rabobab up in the turret, he knocked politely on the door and for good measure pulled the bell-pull.

"Otherwise Occupied!" bawled the Rabobab leaning out of his turret. "Can't you read the flag? Not only Otherwise Occupied but Very Busy. Very Creative. Very, Very Everything!" shouted the Rabobab. "What's the matter with you? Can't you get your whiskers in again?"

"Oh, they're inning and outing just as usual, your Honour," Finnegan called up. "Always a new beginning to life and to my whiskers, your Honour," he added, sitting himself on the doorstep (a great slab of sandstone) by way of suggesting to the Rabobab that he had, temporarily, stopped going round and round.

"Well be off with you then, Finnegan!" cried the Rabobab. "Come back when I'm bored."

"The love-light was particularly beautiful last night," Finnegan remarked, stretching out his legs.

The Rabobab leaned over his turret and considered pouring a ladle of light over Finnegan's head and dissolving him off the doorstep, but decided against it. Finnegan was useful.

"Umm. You think so?" he said.

"Oh yes," replied Finnegan. "Particularly fine. I expect some good dreams and songs will be the result of it today."

"Humph!" said the Rabobab, and between them there was a long silence while Finnegan's whiskers went in and out and the light in the vats bubbled and gurgled.

"There's a bit of a problem with Awesome Bird," said Finnegan stroking his temporarily de-whiskered chin.

The Rabobab almost fell out of his turret with temper. The fierce look in the Rabobab's eyes might have frightened the life out of anyone who didn't know that he could always begin again.

"The Awesome Bird is a fine and beautiful bird!" announced the Rabobab hurrying down the stairs to glare at Finnegan.

"He is indeed a fine and beautiful bird," repeated Finnegan alarmed and walking backwards.

"He is the most beautiful creature ever created on this Island," said the Rabobab jabbing at Finnegan with his ladle.

"It would take your eyes to see that," said Finnegan diplomatically for he preferred the children himself.

"My eyes being a great deal better than your eyes," said the Rabobab.

"Just so," said Finnegan. "And who is to question the eyes of love, your Honour?" he asked, backing still further from the advancing ladle.

"You're beating around the bush," said the Rabobab. "Going round and round and round things."

"It's how I am," said Finnegan apologetically.

"And don't I know that?" shouted the Rabobab, jumping up in the air with rage and going into a kind of spasm of hopping.

"Of course you do, of course you do," said Finnegan soothingly and circling round the Rabobab to avoid the wildly waving ladle.

"Well speak straight for once," howled the Rabobab. "Begin again!"

Finnegan's poor whiskers went in and out at twice their usual speed at this command. And even then, even with this great effort, he couldn't quite bring himself to come directly to the point and to say, outright, that Awesome Bird had brought the wrong child to the Island: that Awesome Bird was poorly.

"It's as I was saying," he began. "Awesome Bird seems – seems – well a bit confused – a bit muddled."

"Strong, swift, white and wonderful!" pronounced the Rabobab. "That is my Awesome Bird."

"Yes, yes, that's true, indeed it is," agreed Finnegan. "But a bit muddled too."

"Never muddled!" declared the Rabobab. "Muddle is unknown to Awesome Bird."

"Have you seen him lately?" inquired Finnegan. "Have you visited him?"

"Me? Visited him?" cried the Rabobab, outraged. "Me? Climb up that darn great tree? Are you out of your mind, Finnegan? Awesome Bird comes to me. Whenever I call, which I haven't done lately, but that is quite, quite, quite beside the point."

"I haven't explained myself very well," said Finnegan. "Let me begin again."

"Please don't!" said the Rabobab. "I've love-light curdling in the vats while you ramble on. Just go. Now! At once! Away with you! Be on your rounds!" And the Rabobab began to hop up to his turret again.

"But your Honour," cried Finnegan, so desperate now that he was forced to speak his mind almost plainly. "It's urgent! Awesome Bird has made a terrible mistake!"

From up above there was a noise as of drums being beaten as the Rabobab banged on his various vats with his ladles and spoons as if each was a gong. Several pineapples, one melon and a basket of oleander petals were flung down on Finnegan's head.

"A mistake?" screeched the Rabobab. "My Awesome Bird make a mistake? Never-never-never! Be off with you, Finnegan, before I pour this vat over your head and then you'll be utterly sozzled and silly with love – perfectly *melted* – and you wouldn't like that, would you?"

"No . . . no, I wouldn't," said Finnegan (who many years ago, in his youth, had been just so afflicted). He climbed back on his donkey and hurried down the path away from the Rabobab's turret, but calling as he went – for it was easier to be brave from a distance – "But it's true, your Honour. Awesome Bird *has* made a mistake. You just ask him! You just visit his nest or call him to yours – I mean your tower. You see instead of a Ginger, who is ours, we've got a Halvie . . . You'll have to do something . . . your Honour . . . your Honour . . . your Honour."

Finnegan's voice faded into the distance.

CHAPTER 20

♫

Laurie's Song

It was dusk when Laurie reached the Palace of Songs and Dreams. The Palace stood in silent semi-darkness against the sunset-red sky. Only two lights glowed – the light in the Book-Keeper's dome and the light in Janni Bean's kitchen.

Laurie made for the kitchen first.

"Still faded, I see," said Janni, ruffling Laurie's hair.

"I think it might be a *little* gingery – here and there," said Laurie.

"Ummm!" said Janni, giving him a sharp glance. "Well, we shall see. You better have a marmalade sandwich and a slice of ginger cake," and she rolled out the big tin and cut him a fat slice.

Laurie sat at the table and ate. How long, he wondered, could one go on eating ginger cake and *not* turn ginger?

"I hear you're song-making tonight," said Janni. "Best not to do that on an empty stomach. Another slice?"

"No thank you," said Laurie, gazing longingly at a tray of pale blonde sugary biscuits.

"Oh, not those," said Janni, following his gaze. "They might fade you even more."

"I better be off to the Book-Keeper then," said Laurie.

"Good song-making," said Janni. "I'm making some extra strong marmalade tonight."

Laurie managed a faded smile.

The cable car had been switched off for the night. The bucket seats swung eerily down the hallway of the Palace. Laurie climbed the stairs to the dome.

"Oh, there you are," said the Book-Keeper. "I've a studio ready for you and Niko here is going to help you." Niko was a small, sturdy Rabobab child. Like Gwen he was a music apprentice and he had seaweedy curls, like Gwen's (only tidier) and a face that was more freckles than face.

All three of them went down to a studio on the third floor. Two musical staves – ten lines of what, to Laurie, looked like fuse wire but was actually the finest silver – were stretched from the wall to the window on a wooden frame with a handle. On a table was a tray of magnetic musical notes – crotchets, quavers, semi-quavers, demi-semi-quavers, semi-demi-semi-quavers and squiggly rests. There was a big curly treble clef and a great rounded bass clef. There were bar lines and time signatures and funny little signs for trills and turns.

"I don't understand *any* of this!" wailed Laurie. "I've only just begun to learn . . . begun to learn . . ." but then he couldn't remember what it was he *had* begun to learn and if it was a piano or a flute or a cello.

"I'm never going to be able to make a song!" cried Laurie, the tears springing to his eyes. (He felt much like the girl shut up in the stable by the king and told to spin flax into gold.)

"Don't worry about that," said the Book-Keeper, settling himself into a rocking chair made, it seemed, to fit his bent shape exactly.

"Niko will do all that for you. That's what he's here for. All you have to do is sing the song."

The Book-Keeper padded some cushions about himself and put his feet up on a stool as if he was in for a long night.

"All!" said Laurie despairingly, for somehow, although he often sang songs to himself (particularly in the bath or when out walking Puddles), his head now felt as empty as a Hallowe'en pumpkin.

The Book-Keeper seemed to understand what Laurie was feeling. "It's good to start that way," he said. "Empty. And look, here are all the scrap-books made in the pool. We use them as prompts, mind-jogglers, heart-throbbers, things to get a song going."

Laurie sat down at a second table that was piled high with scrap-books. (Niko perched on the window sill.) The scrap-books were full of pictures of Down There and notes from the red notebooks – the memories of the Rabo-bab children's visits to the Worldly World.

"To make a new song," instructed the Book-Keeper, "you have first to take what is old. You must think about it very hard. Make a picture of it in your mind. A vivid picture. A picture full of every tiny detail. A picture full of colour. And then you have to add something new. Something that is all your own. And lastly you have to sing it so that other people can see and hear the picture in your mind."

Laurie was looking so pale and faded by now that the Book-Keeper smiled and said, "Don't worry. I think you can do it. You have the look of a Songster to me. There's a rhythm in your walk and a spark in your eyes."

"Even though I'm not ginger!" said Laurie.

"Even though you're not Ginger!" agreed the Book-Keeper, laughing.

Encouraged, Laurie began looking through the scrap-books. Niko hummed a few scales to himself. Outside, the sky above the courtyard had turned black. The moon, sweeping upwards, shone on the criss-cross of silver wires.

Laurie, turning the pages of the scrap-books, saw pictures of forests and rivers, fields and fountains, castles and bungalows, cows and sheep, leopards and lions, mountains and waterfalls, old people from India, children from China, skyscrapers from America, the snowy steppes of Russia.

"It has to be something that moves your heart," said the Book-Keeper, watching him. "A song without heart is no song at all."

And so Laurie began work. It was all far more difficult than he had imagined. To start with, nothing whatsoever seemed to move his heart!

He tried making up a song about a farm. As he sang a phrase, Niko quickly clicked the magnetic notes on to the silver wires. But Laurie knew it was a dull song, a dead song, a song without heart.

"Take it slowly," said the Book-Keeper gently. "See if you get the smallest tingle in your toes when you look at a picture."

"In my toes?" asked Laurie looking down at his feet – he was still wearing his slippers.

"Or your fingers," said the Book-Keeper smiling. "A tingle anywhere, in fact."

Niko swept the notes from the silver wires and they began again.

On and on through the night they worked, with Laurie trying a song about a skyscraper, a song about a waterfall, a school song, a song about fish. And all of them were flat

133

songs, heartless songs, songs that would set no-one's foot tapping; songs no-one could hum or remember.

Now and again the Book-Keeper fell asleep. Now and again Niko, too, fell asleep, still perched on his stool, his head nodding him awake again. Laurie thought that far from turning ginger, his hair would turn white with worry.

"If you make Niko dance," said the Book-Keeper, waking up briefly. "You'll know you're on to something."

Wearily Laurie turned to another scrap-book. He was almost too tired to study the pictures properly. Then he saw it! The picture that was a mind-joggling, heart-throbbing prompt. And he felt it, too! The tingle!

It was indeed very, very small. If the Book-Keeper hadn't told him to wait for it, he might not even have noticed it. It went quickly shivering down the nape of his neck and was gone. The tingle-prompting picture was nothing special. It was just an old spaniel with dark brown eyes lying on a doorstep and waiting to be let in. And of course the spaniel was nothing like Puddles. But a vivid picture of Puddles flashed into Laurie's mind as if all the lights of the Palace had suddenly been switched on. And the memory of Puddles sang in his heart as if his heart itself was a violin, a cello, a flute, a piano – a whole orchestra!

"Got it?" asked the Book-Keeper, seeing the look on Laurie's face.

"Yes," said Laurie cautiously, "I think I have."

"Begin then," said the Book-Keeper urgently. "And keep going."

It was almost dawn when Laurie began singing his heart out. Niko, following Laurie's voice, its ups and downs, highs and lows, slows and quicks, deftly fitted the notes on the big wooden frame.

Laurie sang of Puddles as they had first found him – a bedraggled, frightened puppy. He sang all the ups and downs, flips and flaps of Puddles' ears. He sang (in trills and turns and many demi-semi-quavers) all the different wags of Puddles' question-mark of a tail. He sang a slow movement of Puddles curled at the bottom of his bed; a scherzo of Puddles romping and bounding through the park – Niko paused to dance to this one – and he sang of the special, tail-thumping, welcome home Puddles always gave him.

Niko worked faster and faster, fitting in bar lines and time signatures and rests when there was a pause in Laurie's song. And when Laurie had finished singing his picture of 'The Life and Times of Puddles' (as the song came to be known), he sang of how much he loved him and how home wasn't home without him and lastly of how much he missed him.

"Yes," said the Book-Keeper, who had been awake and listening for the last hour. "That is a new song for it has your heart in it and no-one else's. It's a song that would fit wonderfully into a dream, a doggy dream, a dream for someone who could give a dog a really good home."

Laurie looked at the silver notes glittering on the wires and beamed.

"Put it out to dry and then translate it into dream sound," ordered the Book-Keeper and Niko opened the window onto the courtyard, wound the big handle on the frame and slid Laurie's song out into the light of dawn so that the notes shivered and tinkled.

Exhausted Laurie slumped in his chair. "Will that do?" he asked. "Will the Rabobab hear it? Will he let me stay?"

"It's certainly a song worthy of a Rabobab child," said the Book-Keeper, wiping his eyes, for like many a good song, Laurie's had made him cry. "But you will have to sing it to the Rabobab yourself."

"Oh no!" cried Laurie – for this felt like the last and most scary trial of all and he was beyond-everything tired. "Will you come with me?" he asked. "And please can we take Gwen?"

The Book-Keeper sighed. "I suppose I shall have to," he said. "It's a long time since I left my books. I'm a man of words, not actions, and a meeting with the Rabobab is sure to put me in a twizz for weeks and . . ."

"Please!" begged Laurie. "I'll never do it alone."

But before the Book-Keeper could answer they heard a tremendous rumpus in the courtyard.

CHAPTER 21

Mothers

It was Gwen who found Puddles. While Laurie was making his song, Gwen slept on the beach with the other Rabobab children. But despite the love-light, Gwen slept badly.

Around her the other children were gossiping about invaders and dungeons but Gwen didn't bother to listen. Invaders was a subject the Rabobab children often talked about at night when they wanted to scare each other a bit. They talked about them in much the same way as Worldly children might talk about ghosts or aliens from out of space.

Gwen was too worried about Laurie to listen. Would he be able to make a song? Would it be good enough? Would the Rabobab let him stay? It was hard to keep all this a secret from the other children, yet Gwen did not dare tell anyone about Laurie. And it was hard too, not to talk about the subject that most filled Gwen's sea-weedy head – mothers: the kisses and cuddles of.

So while the other children still slept, Gwen wriggled out of her sleeping bag and went walking up the mountain paths.

Some strangely wise and doggy instinct had made

Puddles search for Laurie while keeping himself hidden from all the children. After all, he had seen Mrs O'Grady, Susan and Ginger dragged off and shut up in what, to Puddles, looked like a very nasty large kennel. The bed of bouncy basil in which he'd curled up for the night was in a hidden hollow just off the mountain path. Only someone who knew the Island well, someone who wanted to walk and think by herself, could have found him there. And that someone was Gwen.

Puddles, of course, didn't recognise Gwen. But instantly he sniffed a smell of Laurie about her. His nose quivered. He opened one eye. Two. His nose went into a semi-demi-semi-quaver of a quiver and then he jumped up, his tail lifting at once into its usual question mark and excitedly he ran round and round her, wagging his question mark and licking her legs.

"So *you're* Puddles!" cried Gwen, laughing.

Lost and lonely as he'd been, Puddles was delighted to hear his name. He rolled over and over and waited for his tummy to be tickled. Then he was back on his four paws again, wagging his tail even harder, running a little away, then coming back again.

"However did you get here?" asked Gwen. "And what are you trying to tell me?" And then she groaned, for it was quite obvious to her that Awesome Bird must have made *another* awesome mistake and that this time the gossip about invaders hadn't been just a scary bedtime story. Had Awesome Bird brought Puddles to the Island instead of some other child? Had he brought Puddles *and* Ginger? Gwen didn't know, but she prepared to follow wherever Puddles might lead her.

It was to the dungeon of the Lighthouse, of course,

and once there, Puddles jumped up and down with such enthusiasm he began to look like a bouncing grey coconut. He was careful not to bark, but he whined and whimpered.

Mrs O'Grady, Susan and Ginger had had an awful night's sleep. They had used old sacks as blankets, but the cold dampness of the dungeon kept them all shivering and more than once during the night Mrs O'Grady had been heard to say, "Oh for my hot water bottle – or for Puddles, who's a hot water bottle in himself."

"Try to sleep," Susan had answered. "In the morning I'm going to try to call out to one of the Rabobab children."

When they heard the noise outside the dungeon, all three of them were awake at once.

"Puddles!" exclaimed Mrs O'Grady, and pulling three boxes to the dungeon door she climbed up and peered through the grille. "Puddles! You're a wonder dog!" she cried.

"And slightly more welcome than Awesome Bird!" said Susan jumping up and down and trying to catch a glimpse of Puddles.

Ginger found some more boxes and climbed up beside Mrs O'Grady.

"Gwen!" he said, stretching his hand through the grille. "I'm back!"

But Gwen at that moment only had eyes for Mrs O'Grady. For a whole minute she gazed silently up at her and then she said, "Are you Laurie's mother?"

"Indeed I am!" said Mrs O'Grady. "And if you know some way of getting us out of here, I should be much obliged. This is Susan. She's another mother."

"Two mothers!" breathed Gwen and in a flash she had

rushed up the stairs to the Lighthouse Keeper's lamp room.

"What do you mean by locking up two mothers?" shouted Gwen down the Lighthouse Keeper's ear – he was just climbing out of his bunk.

The Lighthouse Keeper was so startled he almost lost his footing on the ladder and his wispy white hair stood on end as though electrified.

"Is that Gwen?" he asked, turning his bright blind blue eyes on her. "What are you going on about? Mothers? What mothers?"

"Down in the dungeon," shrieked Gwen. "You've got two mothers locked up *and* my old friend Ginger."

"Invaders," said the Lighthouse Keeper, huddling down in his chair under the force of Gwen's temper. "I was told they were invaders. I remember now. Meant to tell the Book-Keeper. Forgot somehow . . ."

"You forgot?" shouted Gwen.

"Was having such a lovely dream yesterday," said the Lighthouse Keeper apologetically. "And when I'm working the Light, everything else goes out of my mind."

"Invaders are one thing," said Gwen sternly. "Mothers are quite another. And anyway, it's not their fault that they're here. It's the Awesome Bird. He's caused no end of trouble."

"Not the Awesome Bird!" said the Lighthouse Keeper in a tone of the deepest respect. "He can surely do no wrong."

"The Awesome Bird has not been a bit awesome lately," snapped Gwen. "And everyone knows it. Only no-one dares to tell the Rabobab. Now give me the key to the dungeon."

Meekly the Lighthouse Keeper handed over the key.

And in a flash Gwen was off down the stairs. She had to struggle with the huge key, but very soon Mrs O'Grady, Susan and Ginger had stumbled out of the dungeon and were rubbing themselves warm while Puddles so leapt for joy that his question mark turned into an exclamation mark. To Gwen's delight, Mrs O'Grady and Susan gave her the biggest hug she had ever had.

"Do you know where Laurie is?" asked Mrs O'Grady when she had done hugging.

"Yes," said Gwen. "He's making a song in the Palace of Songs and Dreams. Shall I take you there?"

"You're an absolute darling," said Mrs O'Grady. "Yes, please."

So off they set up the cliff path to the Palace.

"Has Laurie done much swimming?" asked Mrs O'Grady.

"Oh lots!" said Gwen happily. ('An absolute darling!' she was saying to herself. 'An absolute darling!')

"We must hurry then," said Mrs O'Grady to Susan. "Goodness knows how much time has been washed off him. It's the third day. He might not even remember me."

But Gwen didn't hear this. She was dancing ahead of them. Gwen had no other thought than that now they would all live happily ever after together and that she, an 'absolute darling' would be the proud owner of not one but two mothers.

* * *

By the time they reached the Palace, the Rabobab children had finished their breakfasts and were streaming

141

out of the cave houses where they ate and, at Snooze Time, slept.

A whole gaggle of them surrounded Mrs O'Grady, Susan, Ginger and Puddles in the courtyard. At first Puddles was the chief attraction until Gwen, in an important voice said, "Stand back! Stand back! We have two mothers here!"

"Mothers, mothers mothers," chanted the Rabobab children standing back and gazing at Mrs O'Grady and Susan. One small Rabobab pinched Susan to see if she was real. Susan squealed.

Janni Bean, hearing the hubbub from the kitchen, came to the back door.

"Oh my jams and jellies!" said Janni. "That wretched Awesome Bird . . . this is the last straw!" And taking off her apron she hurried off to find Finnegan.

Laurie, Niko and the Book-Keeper had been so absorbed in the song that they only slowly became aware of the noise in the courtyard. It was Niko, winding the last notes of Laurie's song out of the window, who cried, "Look! Look! A furry four-legs!"

And then Laurie looked.

You could say that at that moment, Laurie's heart flew out of the window and down down down to Mrs O'Grady and Puddles. Seeing them there, seeing his mother, tired and grubby, her anxious face covered in smuts from the dungeon, and seeing Puddles confused and frightened by so much attention, Laurie knew once and for all where he belonged.

He rushed out of the room so fast that all the notes on the wires jangled behind him. Down the stairs rushed Laurie followed by Niko and the bewildered Book-Keeper.

And when Laurie appeared in the courtyard, Puddles almost knocked him over with delight, bouncing up and down and licking every spare bit of Laurie that could be licked.

"Puddles!" said Laurie. "Oh my dear, dear Puddles. How I've missed you!"

And then Mrs O'Grady burst through the crowd of Rabobab children who surrounded her.

"Laurie B. O'Grady!" she bawled. "Just *where* do you think you've been?"

To the astonishment of the watching children Mrs O'Grady boxed Laurie about the ears.

"Going off on the back of a bird!" she cried. "Don't you ever let me catch you doing that again! I've been worried sick about you!" and then she burst into tears, threw her arms round Laurie and hugged him so hard it was a wonder there was any Laurie left.

"Never say no to an adventure," said Laurie. "I read it in a book."

"There's books and books and adventures and adventures," said Mrs O'Grady, "and I can do without another one for a long, long time. Now where's that nice little girl who brought us here?"

"Gwen," said Laurie. "My best friend, Gwen."

But Gwen had vanished.

All the Rabobab children made a great noise looking for her and calling her until the Book-Keeper climbed on to the step of the fountain and flapped his arms for silence.

"It's time the Rabobab sorted this out," said the Book-Keeper.

"I should jolly well think so," said Mrs O'Grady, who had recovered something of her old dragon spirit.

"Please will *you* take us?" asked Laurie.

The Book-Keeper heaved a great sigh. "I suppose I'll have to," he said.

"I want an immediate flight home!" demanded Mrs O'Grady.

The Book-Keeper looked at Mrs O'Grady sadly. "I'm afraid there is no knowing what the Rabobab will do – or say," he said. "And almost everything will depend on his mood – that and Laurie's song."

CHAPTER 22

The Book-Keeper's Letter

All the Rabobab children followed the Book-Keeper. They made a long winding procession up the mountain path singing as they walked. But when the Rabobab's towers came into view they fell silent.

Laurie, Mrs O'Grady, Susan and Ginger had agreed to stay quietly at the back of the procession though it had been difficult to persuade Mrs O'Grady not to march at the front.

The Book-Keeper, at the head of the procession, walked slowly. He was not used to being away from his books and he didn't much like it. In addition, he had spent so many years bent over his books that it was not easy for him to straighten up.

"I'm not a man of action," complained the Book-Keeper to the nearest child. "I'm a man of words."

"Nice words," said the child, smiling, but this didn't cheer the Book-Keeper who at that moment was wishing he'd never set eyes on Laurie.

For his part the Rabobab was very put out to see the Book-Keeper and the children slowly but certainly climbing towards him. He knew perfectly well that only something very serious could drag the Book-Keeper away from his books and he feared it was more bad news about his beloved Awesome Bird – news that he didn't wish to hear.

Hastily the Rabobab closed his shutters and hung a sign on his front door knob. 'Very Out' it said.

The Book-Keeper came to a stop before this sign and turned it round the other way so that it read 'Very In'. Then he sat down on the doorstep and thought.

The Book-Keeper was famous for his Thoughts (many of them recorded in a special volume) and the Rabobab children knew that when 'In Thought', the Book-Keeper was not to be disturbed. They made a silent circle round him and waited.

As instructed, Laurie and the others hid behind a rock.

"I'll write the Rabobab a letter," said the Book-Keeper at last. He felt very pleased with this idea. Anything on paper pleased the Book-Keeper. He dug about in his pockets until he found pen and paper. The Rabobab children all sighed and decided it was Snooze Time.

"Really," whispered Mrs O'Grady from behind the rock. "I'm sure I could handle this better myself."

"Leave it to the Book-Keeper," advised Susan. "I think he knows what he's doing."

"And I've things I want to ask you," said Laurie.

"Ah yes," said Susan, "I'm sure there are. I expect you want to know about being a Halvie."

"Yes," said Laurie. "Before . . . before the Awesome Bird brought me here, I overheard you and Mum talking. You spoke of the kiss of life and the Island – this Island, though I didn't know it then."

And so Mrs O'Grady told Laurie the story of the car accident in the far north of Scotland and of how Laurie's father had been killed and Laurie himself only just saved by the arrival of Susan.

"There was nothing I could do for your father," said Susan. "And I hesitated about you – knowing that it wouldn't be just life I was breathing into you but – well, dreams and songs, the spirit of the Island. I knew there was a danger. A danger that you would never feel quite at home in the world. That you might suffer hankerings, yearnings ... and never understand what they were about."

"But we hoped," said Mrs O'Grady. "We hoped you'd grow out of them ..."

"Only I didn't," said Laurie in a very small voice. "Which is why I don't belong anywhere. Why I'm a Halvie."

Mrs O'Grady wiped her eyes with the edge of her kimono and put an arm round Laurie to comfort him. But Susan fluffed out her petticoats (much like Awesome Bird fluffing his feathers) and grew brisk.

"There's no need to feel sorry for yourself. You should count yourself lucky," she said, so that Laurie looked up at her, surprised. "Being a Halvie *doesn't* mean that you don't belong anywhere. It simply means that you belong to two worlds. There are many Halvies down on earth. Not all of them are foster mothers like me ..."

"You're a Halvie, too?" asked Laurie.

"Of course," said Susan, giving him her most warming smile. "You can always recognise a Halvie," she continued. "They're the glinting people."

"Glinting?" repeated Laurie.

"People who catch the light," said Susan. "And without them the Worldly World would be very, very grey."

"But will the Rabobab send me home or keep me here?" asked Laurie.

"Keep you here?" cried Mrs O'Grady. "If that Rabobab thinks he can ..."

But Susan laid a gentle hand on her shoulder. "That's one question I can't answer, Laurie," she said. "Why don't you and Ginger go and explore a little. Goodness knows how long it will take the Book-Keeper to write his letter."

"We could build a cairn," said Laurie. "Like mountaineers do when they've climbed a particularly high mountain. To show they've been there."

So that's what they did. It felt strange being together again, not on the bank above the railway line of Umberton Road, but high in the mountains, in the bright crisp air of Rabobab Island, with the sea shining below them.

If I go home, thought Laurie, I might never see Ginger again.

"You won't forget me," said Ginger, as if reading Laurie's thoughts. "Because really you've *been* me for the last few days. You've been living *my* life."

"I suppose I have," said Laurie. "In a faded kind of way. And now I'd rather like my own back. You've no idea how much ginger cake Janni Bean has made me eat!"

Ginger laughed. Together they built a very satisfactory cairn. Susan and Mrs O'Grady were kept well occupied by a succession of small Rabobab children who came for a cuddle.

The Book-Keeper, bent over his page, scribbled on.

Dear Sir, Dear Great Rabobab, Dear You-Up-In-A-Tower, Dear Catcher of Love-light, Dear Maestro, wrote the Book-Keeper.

I am a man of words, not actions. My job is to see that all the songs and dreams created on the Island are recorded in volumes, alphabetically and illustrated when necessary.

"*It is true, of course, that I hold the records of all Rabobab children plus the dates on which they visit There and when they are to return to Here. Clearly then, it is I, more than anyone else on the Island who is able to recognise when we have invaders. Even so I do not see it as part of my job specifications to do anything about it.*

You should have employed someone else. Might I suggest an Ombudsman? This is a very nice word and I expect he would have been a great asset to the Island, going about singing Om-Om-Om which is, I believe, what Ombudsmen do. But I digress. You should have employed someone else to deal with the likes of O'Grady and Puddles (a very peculiar creature if I may say so and we have never seen the likes of him here on the Island).

We have a Halvie in our midst. A boy called Laurie. We have a Ginger too and Ginger belongs Here and Laurie There and Someone – or Some Bird – has got them muddled up. I don't say this myself. I am only telling you what others say. It is all too much for me, I can tell you. All I want to do is keep my records straight and there is a new song which I was half-way through putting in the records when all this happened.

Anyway, the aforementioned O'Grady, Puddles, someone called Susan and the Ginger-Laurie boys are A Cause of Great Worry. (The Book-Keeper liked using capital letters). *The Halvie has written a very beautiful song. I think you should hear it.*

Well it is all up to you now.

With many respectful greetings and saving Your Grace,

BK

P.S. I expect it's all the fault of the Awesome Bird. Awesome seems quite the wrong word for him. Daft would be better.

The Rabobab, squinting through a crack in his front

door sat on his doormat and waited for the letter to plop through his letter box which, after a considerable while, it did.

He liked the opening very much and he liked the respectful greetings and the saving of His Grace. But the middle made him do a lot of hopping about and when he got to the P.S. he was so angry that he flung open the door and nearly knocked the Book-Keeper over.

All the children woke up at once. Mrs O'Grady, peeping over the rock saw, at last, the strange, wild figure of the Rabobab. A hopping mad Rabobab.

"Oh my!" said Mrs O'Grady, and sat down again in a hurry. Laurie and Ginger crept back to look at the Rabobab. Laurie went very pale. Ginger smiled and said, "Just as he ever was!"

The Rabobab had put on his finest robe. It was made of strips of violet and purple, plum and scarlet silks. (The colours reminded Laurie of Janni's jams.)

Out of his tower came the Rabobab with all his silks fluttering and flying about him so that he looked as if he might take off at any minute and fly like a small and multi-coloured awesome Rabobab.

"The Awesome Bird is truly awesome!" bellowed the Rabobab.

The Book-Keeper, knocked off the doorstep, lost his nerve entirely.

"The Awesome Bird is truly awesome," he repeated at once.

"Truly awesome. Truly awesome," murmured the children as a chorus.

"Humph!" said the Rabobab, the wind taken out of his robe and his temper. "Well, that's all that needs to be said. Go away! I've work to do. You're a very good Book-Keeper. Go and look after the books!"

And with that the Rabobab turned on his heel, went back into his tower and slammed the door.

"But Great Rabobab, dear, dear Great Sir," pleaded the Book-Keeper through the letterbox. "What shall we do with the Halvie and the Worldly Ones?"

"Melt 'em!" the Rabobab shouted through the letter box. "Dissolve them into light. They'll be much happier that way and so shall we. I'll see to it tonight. Be off with you!"

"Well, that does it," said Mrs O'Grady rising from behind her rock. "If he thinks he can dissolve *me* into light, he's got another think coming!" And she was about to march forward and hammer on the Rabobab's door.

"Wait," said the Book-Keeper, holding her back. "He'll calm down in a while. If the children sing to him it will be soothing. And then I'll try again."

"All right," said Mrs. O'Grady reluctantly. "But if all this singing and soothing doesn't work, I'm going to give him a piece of my mind. He's yet to meet a true O'Grady!"

★ ★ ★

Janni Bean guessed where to find Finnegan. He had gone back to see the Awesome Bird. And it was there, under the eucalyptus tree that Janni found Finnegan, sitting sadly on the ground and not even singing his whiskers song.

"Things are terrible at the Palace," said Janni, getting off her donkey and sitting beside Finnegan. "Not only has he . . . " (Janni rolled her eyes upwards to indicate the Awesome Bird) "brought the wrong child, but now we've got two mothers, and a Puddles. At least we have Ginger back. But they've all gone off to the Rabobab."

"I doubt he'll listen," said Finnegan gloomily. "I've already tried. He's in a terrible mood because the love-level is so low Down There and nothing seems to lift it."

"And how about AB up there?" asked Janni.

"Worse," said Finnegan. "See for yourself."

Unlike Finnegan, Janni Bean was very nimble. She climbed swiftly up the tree to the Awesome Bird's nest.

The Awesome Bird was dozing. His feathers looked limp and grey. Their aquamarine tips no longer shone and gleamed.

Awesome Bird was feeling very poorly. Indeed he had felt very poorly for a long time and no-one (so it seemed to him) had taken any notice. They had simply expected him to carry on being awesome. It is a very hard thing being awesome all the time with never a day off. And it is very lonely.

For a long time Awesome Bird had thrived on the Rabobab's love and admiration. Being called 'My Beauty' by the Rabobab was very uplifting both to the spirit and the wings. And being the Rabobab's messenger gave him an importance he had rejoiced in.

But being a messenger, carrying children to and fro (with hardly ever a thank you), visiting the Worldly World and seeing dreams neglected and dreams thrown away – all this was very gloomy work indeed. Being awe-some simply seemed to mean that people kept their distance. As the Rabobab's messenger he was admired, adored. For himself, for his large and lonely self, Awe-some Bird felt unwanted and rejected and Very Put Out.

Though nobody seemed to have noticed, there were one or two Rabobab children he hadn't even bothered to de-liver. His Worldly geography had gone so awry that he couldn't be bothered to remember if Washington was in

America or Russia; Paris in England or France. And as for his flight times . . . They were, to say the least, erratic.

Worst of all was the Awesome Bird's fear that if he should tell any of this to the Rabobab, the Rabobab might fall out of love with him. Find another messenger. Retire him. Make him redundant. And what sort of life is that for a once-awesome bird?

Janni Bean, peering in at the nest where the Awesome Bird lay with his head tucked under his wing and his usually conker-dark eyes looking pale and dull, could know nothing of Awesome Bird's feelings. But she was a very practical woman. She took one look at him, whisked a thermometer out of her apron and stuck it under Awesome Bird's wing. Awesome Bird didn't protest, didn't even turn his head.

Janni Bean slithered down the tree very fast.

"What we have is a very sick Awesome Bird," she said. "His spirits have sunk lower than my thermometer can register. Come on, Finnegan. Let's hurry."

"Where are we going?" asked Finnegan.

"To the Rabobab, of course," said Janni.

"But he won't listen!" said Finnegan.

"I don't suppose he listened to you," said Janni impatiently. "You probably spoke in such a roundabout way, he wouldn't know what you were on about. And as for the Book-Keeper – he'll be so wordy and clever the Rabobab will just get very cross."

"So you think he'll listen to you?" asked Finnegan.

"Who provides him with his favourite apricot jam?" asked Janni. "And his favourite lemon and lime pies?"

"Umm," said Finnegan, "You've got something there."

"I certainly have," said Janni Bean.

CHAPTER 23

♫

Laurie and the Rabobab

Finnegan and Janni found Gwen sobbing on the beach her arms wound round her knees, her tangle of sea-weedy curls hiding her face.

"Heigh-up," said Finnegan. "Here's sorrow unknown on the Island. And from one who always says 'Merry morning' in the merriest of ways."

Gwen looked up at Finnegan through a tangle of curls and tears.

"Is it something a jam tart won't fix?" asked Janni producing one from her pocket. (Janni had the notion that almost anything could be fixed by jam of one sort or another.)

Gwen shook her head at the tart.

"We had a pledge," she sobbed, "Laurie and I. He was going to be my friend forever and ever and now he's found his mother and he won't want to stay and his mother cuddles and hugs him and says 'Don't, don't, don't'. And I want a mother too!"

And with that Gwen buried her head in her knees and began a fresh bout of sobbing.

"Come along with us," said Finnegan. "We're on our way to the Rabobab. There's more to be sorted out here than ever I thought."

So Gwen climbed on the back of Finnegan's donkey and rested her head against his warm round back and listened to him singing and watched his whiskers ining and outing and although it wasn't quite as good as a hug from Mrs O'Grady, it was very comforting.

When they reached the Rabobab's tower, the children were still singing their soothing song. The Book-Keeper and Mrs O'Grady had fallen asleep back-to-back. Ginger and Susan were dancing together.

Janni jumped off her donkey, gave the Book-Keeper a kick to wake him up, marched directly to the Rabobab's door and hammered on it with her strong cook's fist.

The Rabobab flung open a shutter.

"Now what?" he yelled. "Has everyone decided to annoy me today?"

Janni Bean wasted neither words nor time. "The Awesome Bird is ill," she said. "His spirit has sunk to the lowest low tide."

"Ill?" cried the Rabobab rushing outside. "My Beauty, my Awesome Bird. Ill? Why has nobody told me?"

"Well, if you don't mind my saying so, Sir . . . " began Finnegan.

"I do mind!" snapped the Rabobab. "I mind a lot."

"I was trying to explain in my letter, as best I could, as tactfully as I could, and with the very best use of words that . . . " began the Book-Keeper.

"Pah!" said the Rabobab. "I must go and see My Beauty at once. His spirit lower than the lowest tide, you say?"

"Hold on," said Janni, grabbing a purple flap of the Rabobab's floating silks. "You've a few other things to sort out first."

"You're not going to bother me with these invaders are

you?" cried the Rabobab. "I've given my instruction. Melt 'em! Dissolve them into light. Is that one of them over there?" (He was looking at Mrs O'Grady.) "She'd make quite good light and I'm a bit short today."

"I have some particularly beautiful apricot jam at the moment," said Janni. "Spread on a scone it is quite out of this planet. Sweet yet tangy. Tastes like sunshine."

"Umm," said the Rabobab, hesitating.

"And then there's the gooseberry," continued Janni. "Never been a finer year for gooseberry. Pale as a new leaf, sharp as sea-spray."

"Oh very well then," said the Rabobab rather sulkily. "What do you want me to do?"

"Send me and my Laurie home, please," interrupted Mrs O'Grady, unable to keep silent a moment longer. "That bird of yours brought Laurie here by mistake. Please don't melt us. I'm sure neither of us would make very good light."

"No," agreed the Rabobab. "Now that I look at you properly, I think you'd be rather murky."

Susan, Ginger and Puddles all crept fowards behind Mrs O'Grady.

Puddles tried a tentative lick of the Rabobab's hand. The Rabobab looked very surprised, then he knelt down and ceremoniously licked Puddles' nose in return. Nobody dared laugh.

The Rabobab stood up and surveyed the anxious group in front of him.

"Well, well, well," he said, walking all round Laurie. "A Halvie. And quite a nice specimen."

"Don't you go calling my son a specimen," began Mrs O'Grady, but Susan hushed her.

"And Susan," said the Rabobab. "What are you doing Here? Your job is Down There, as well you know."

"Please Sir, I came to help my friend," said Susan. "I've been looking after your child – Ginger. It was Ginger the Awesome Bird, your most beautiful bird, should have returned. If he wasn't so poorly, I'm sure he'd have got it right."

"Of course he would!" said the Rabobab. "No question about it. Well then, this is the rule." (The Rabobab was prone to making up rules as and when it pleased him.) "If a Halvie *should* come to the Island, we have to decide where his heart truly belongs. Have you got a song, boy?"

The Book-Keeper bustled up. "Oh yes, Sir, Great Sir, please Your Maestro – he spent all night with me in the studio making his song and I do assure you that as songs go . . ."

"Any minute now you'll be writing me another letter," said the Rabobab. "Let us hear the song and then I shall know whether Laurie is to stay Here or go back There."

And so, as all the Rabobab children gathered round, as Mrs O'Grady anxiously clutched Susan's hand, as Finnegan put an arm round the tearful Gwen and as the Rabobab sat on his doorstep to listen, Laurie began.

He sang 'The Life and Times of Puddles' – the wag of his tail, the cold of his nose, the ups and downs of his ears, his flump on the bed, his hot-water-bottle warmth. Second time round, the song grew a little, as songs will.

Perched on a rock, his head thrown back, Laurie sang his heart out.

But what the Rabobab and all those listening heard was not 'The Life and Times of Puddles', but a homesick song, a sad and Worldly song, but a song with so much love in it that even the Rabobab had to wipe away a tear.

There was a moment's silence when Laurie had finished. Mrs O'Grady held Laurie close as if she thought she might lose him that very minute.

"I'd quite like to keep you . . . " the Rabobab began slowly, "for you sing a fine song but it's perfectly clear that . . . " (everyone held their breath) "you belong Down There."

The sigh of relief from everyone was like the low hush of the wind on the sea.

"But," said the Rabobab, holding up his hand for silence, and looking at Laurie with his fierce sea-coloured eyes, "Halvies have work to do Down There."

"Yes Sir," said Laurie.

"Always stay open to the light," ordered the Rabobab, "and make songs. Sing."

"Yes Sir," repeated Laurie grinning from ear to ear.

Mrs O'Grady was so delighted she rushed forward and gave the Rabobab a big hug.

The Rabobab pushed her away in alarm. "Mothers!" said the Rabobab. "I can't be doing with them."

And as he said this, and as all the Rabobab children began dancing, there was the sound of someone crying.

"Now what?" demanded the Rabobab. "Is there no end to my troubles today?"

"If you please Sir, if you wouldn't mind just waiting an extra moment," said Finnegan. "It's young Gwen here."

"It's all my fault," burst out Laurie. "I gave her my pledge to stay forever and be her friend and she so badly wants a mother of her own . . . Sir."

"I see," said the Rabobab, looking down at Gwen who Finnegan had pushed before him.

"Book-Keeper – when is this child due an earth visit."

"Well, from memory Sir, and when I checked my records yesterday, or no, not yesterday, the day before yesterday, I think it is a week Wednesday."

"Put it forward," ordered the Rabobab. "And you,

boy," he said, turning to Laurie, "a pledge is a pledge. Wherever you are – Here or There – you will remain Gwen's true friend. Is that understood?"

"Absolutely Sir," said Laurie.

"In the meantime," the Rabobab said to Gwen, "when you're home on the Island, Ginger will be your special friend."

"I suppose you were my *first* friend," Gwen said reluctantly. Ginger grinned. "And I'm Here for good," he said. "I'll be waiting when you get back."

"And Down There," whispered Mrs O'Grady to Gwen, "you won't just have Susan for a mother, you'll have me too!"

"And now," said the Rabobab, "I must go to my poor, poor, Awesome Bird. Follow me. I think he needs everyone."

CHAPTER 24

The Awesome Bird

For the Rabobab to leave his tower was such a rare event that it was like a holiday for the children – a day off from their work in the Palace.

Finnegan and Janni Bean left their donkeys tethered and joined in the parade that followed the Rabobab down the hillside. Several Rabobab children held the silky flaps of the Rabobab's robe as if he were a bride going to a wedding.

Mrs O'Grady's usual optimism had returned. Now, at last, she felt, they were getting somewhere. The Rabobab would restore the Awesome Bird to health and soon she, Laurie, Susan and Puddles would be on their way home.

Only Laurie and the Rabobab looked miserable, and Susan uncertain. The Rabobab, of course, was worried about the Awesome Bird's well-being. Laurie was worried about his memory.

"My time is almost up," he whispered to Susan. "They say it takes three days for your memory to fade here. And look, there's a faint bluebird mark coming on my arm."

Susan looked. There was indeed a faint blue picture appearing on the top of Laurie's arm.

"Try not to worry," she whispered back – for neither of

them wanted to alarm Mrs O'Grady – "trust the Rabo-bab."

"Could you just remind me of my address," pleaded Laurie.

"Flat 6, Block B, Clampitt Court, Umberton Road, Rodwell," Susan whispered back.

"Thank you!" Laurie said gratefully.

Down the mountain paths, all along the beach with its beautiful sands and foamy waves they walked, up through the hills carpeted in wild flowers and all so beautiful that Laurie wondered how he could ever want to leave it. But he knew the answer. It wasn't home.

At last they reached the eucalyptus tree. The Rabobab climbed aloft a boulder facing the Awesome Bird's nest and prepared to make a speech. Everyone else sat down.

"This is Rabobab Island," began the Rabobab, spreading his arms wide to include the children who crept nearer to listen. "And I am the Great Rabobab." He waited for applause.

"It is Here that all new thoughts have their beginning," continued the Rabobab. "It is Here that the light is brewed in the vats and wells of my tower. It is Here light is turned into love and, as you know, love is the essential ingredients of the songs and dreams which you work so hard on making in the Palace.

"From Here we send our dearly beloved Rabobab children to spend time Down There, learning the ways of the Worldly Ones so that we, in our songs and dreams may know best how to speak to them. And all our children are gathered in again, like the harvest, brought home to the Island and to Happily Ever After. And who – apart from my Great Self of course – works hardest for us all?"

It was clear to everyone by now that the Rabobab was

trying to rouse the Awesome Bird by the grandeur of his speech and all eyes looked upwards to the big twiggy nest of the bird which seemed to be overflowing with song scraps, Rabobab Orders and many feathers. Every now and again a song scrap would drift, kite-like, gently down to earth.

"Why, Awesome Bird, of course!" announced the Rabobab in his grandest voice and waving his arms to encourage further applause. "Awesome Bird it is who carries our beloved children from Here to There and There to Here. How much we love and appreciate him," continued the Rabobab in full flattering throttle and throwing his voice up to the top of the tree. "How dear he is to us all! Three zings for Awesome Bird!"

(They do not have cheers on Rabobab Island, they have zings, and the children responded to the Rabobab's plea with a sound passed from one to the other which echoed across the Island like the ting of a thousand triangles.)

There was a long silence during which everyone looked up expectantly at the Awesome Bird's nest, but all they heard were a few hiccups and a rustle. More feathers and scraps floated down on their heads.

Immensely sad, the Rabobab sat down on the boulder. Apart from the tear shed over Laurie's song, he had not cried for a few thousand years, but now all the children saw two silver tears glide down his cheeks.

"Without my messenger," said the Rabobab, "we are all doomed."

It was then that Ginger stepped forward.

"Please Sir, please Great Rabobab, would you let me climb up and talk to the Awesome Bird. I think I'm quite good with birds."

Ginger was remembering something Susan had told

him. How it wasn't good for the Awesome Bird to be treated as Awesome all the time. How he needed a bit of looking after and someone to keep him in order, and how dejected he grew when no-one said thank you.

"Let the boy try," urged Finnegan.

"Can't do any harm," added the Book-Keeper.

"Awesome Bird needs a boy of his own," said Janni Bean, "I've thought so for a long time."

Despairingly the Rabobab shrugged. "Very well then," he said. "Though never before has My Beauty refused to respond to me. Here, take this phial of special light. Sprinkle it on the tips of his wings. It may do something."

Everyone watched as Ginger climbed the tree. Its branches were set wide and Ginger had to haul himself up, stretching his arms as far as they would go.

Laurie, watching him, thought how naturally Ginger climbed. It was as if this was what he was *meant* to do. Ginger's feet were large but nimble. The size of them seemed to allow him to balance steadily on the boughs of the old tree. He was skinny and bendy too, so that as he got higher it looked as if he was not so much climbing the tree, but weaving his body in and out of the branches. This is what Ginger's good at, thought Laurie. And what I'm good at is making songs. And the last trace of jealousy vanished from his heart.

Ginger disappeared in the leafy foliage at the top of the tree. Down below everyone waited.

The Awesome Bird pretended to be asleep. Ginger made no effort to wake him from this pretend sleep, he just began quietly chatting to himself and, at the same time, tidying up the nest, clearing away a few song scraps, doing a little grooming of Awesome Bird's dishevelled feathers and sprinkling the phial of light on the tips of the Bird's wings.

"Hello, my beauty," said Ginger, using the Rabobab's term but in a much less grand and more friendly way. "My, you've had a hard time of it of late, I can see that. Particularly with no-one to help you. I'm sorry I didn't come sooner really. But I'm here now. And I'll just tidy up a bit if you don't mind. Oh look, there's a few honeyed peanuts here you seem to have missed. Perhaps you'd like them now?"

The Awesome Bird opened one eye at this and when he thought Ginger wasn't looking, pecked at a few nuts.

"All these old Orders you're sitting on," said Ginger. "If you just moved over a bit, I could make you much more comfortable."

The Awesome Bird did as he was told. Ginger removed more crumpled scraps and fluffed up the feathers and moss of the nest. When all this was done, and the liquid light from the Rabobab's phial had been sprinkled on the aquamarine tips of his wings, Awesome Bird looked a great deal brighter. Ginger sat astride a bough and Bird and boy considered each other.

"I'd guess it's rather lonely being awesome," said Ginger. "Very grand, but very lonely. From now on, I'll try and help you."

The Awesome Bird gazed at Ginger with a brown and dreamy gaze. The greyness of his feathers was disappearing by the minute. Soon they were white as newly washed sheets and the tips began to gleam and glow.

"Everyone's missing you," continued Ginger. "And nobody really minds that you've made a few mistakes."

Tentatively Ginger stretched out a hand and stroked Awesome Bird. "Appreciation," said Ginger. "That's what you need."

The Awesome Bird stirred softly under Ginger's hand.

Being stroked made a great change from children clutching him as he flew from Here to There and There to Here.

"There's rather a special job for you to do," said Ginger. "If you feel up to it that is," he added hastily, for the Awesome Bird had tucked his head under his wing again.

"Those Worldly Ones you brought – Laurie and Mrs O'Grady and my very dear earth mother, Susan – they all need to be taken back again. And of course there's Puddles . . ."

The Awesome Bird shuddered at the mention of Puddles. Ginger hurried on. "And there's little Gwen. She's my special friend now. And it's time for her visit to There."

The Awesome Bird shifted uneasily in his tidy nest.

"Please!" said Ginger, stroking the Bird's head some more. "To show we're friends?"

The Awesome Bird wriggled and jiggled a while and then, to Ginger's vast relief, he stood up, spread wide his wings and making a wonderfully circular flight in the air flew down to the Rabobab's feet.

"Oh, My Beauty!" said the Rabobab. "I've loved you without understanding you. From now on, you will always have Ginger to look after you. And you can be awesome from Monday to Saturday, and perfectly ordinary on Sunday."

"What day is it today?" Mrs O'Grady asked Susan urgently.

"Monday," grinned Susan.

"Thank goodness!" said Mrs O'Grady.

* * *

It took the Awesome Bird two flights to carry Mrs O'Grady, Laurie and Puddles (first) and then Susan and Gwen (second).

The Rabobab children waved them off.

"Always friends!" said Ginger to Laurie. "Here and There!"

"Always friends!" agreed Laurie.

The last Laurie saw of the Island was the fiery spark of Ginger's ginger head and his arm with the bluebird tattoo, waving and waving and waving.

★ ★ ★

Arriving home in Umberton Road in the middle of the night felt as strange as landing on another planet! The block of flats that had seemed so dull looked (with one or two lights glowing in the windows) like a vast and magical ship. Even in the darkness Laurie saw that the sycamore trees had a sheen he had never noticed before. And he could see tall grasses shifting and shimmering down by the railway line and they looked, to him, more beautiful than any of the flowers he had seen on the Island. Even the rain seemed a new delight.

"Sea-spray from the sky!" exclaimed Gwen in astonishment when she and Susan landed – with the Awesome Bird's usual flump and flop – near the yellow van with its blue octopus swirls and its little striped tin chimney.

"Rain!" said Laurie laughing. "It's called rain! Look, you've got lots and lots of it in your hair."

Then Gwen shook her seaweedy tangle so that all the rain drops shone around her.

"I think I'm going to like it There," she said.

"You mean Here," said Susan. "And it's way past your

bedtime, Gwen. It's time to tuck you up and give you a goodnight kiss."

"Is that what mothers always do?" asked Gwen.

"It certainly is," said Susan.

"And will I see you in the morning?" Gwen asked Laurie as Susan opened the door of the van and lit the lamp inside.

"Pledge!" said Laurie.

"Pledge!" said Gwen.

The Awesome Bird, perched briefly on the roof of the van, then he spread wide his wings and took off. They all stood and watched, gazing up at the starry, Worldly sky until he was out of sight. All except Puddles. With his four paws on solid ground again, Puddles made straight for the flats and was there, at the door of number 6, wagging and waiting as Laurie and his mother climbed wearily up the stairs.

A few letters lay on the mat. Half-asleep, Mrs O'Grady opened one.

"Would you believe it," she said. "I've won a holiday on the island of Majorca!"

"Forget it," said Laurie, yawning. "Let's stay home."

"Well maybe for now," said Mrs O'Grady. "But what was it you said on the Island – 'Never say no to an adventure?'"

"Right now I wouldn't say no to my own bed and a mug of hot chocolate," said Laurie.

And very soon that's where he was. In his own bed, with the hot-water bottle that was Puddles curled up at the bottom of it and the hot chocolate only half drunk because Laurie fell asleep before he could finish it.

"Tomorrow," Laurie said sleepily to Puddles, "I'll make up a coming home song." And as he snuggled down under his duvet he noticed that the faint bluebird tattoo had turned bright blue and shone on his arm as though painted there with luminous paint. Laurie grinned in the darkness, knowing now that he would never forget the Island, Ginger, the Rabobab and the Awesome Bird and knowing too that it was all right to belong to two worlds, to Here and to There.

"Stay open to the light," Laurie murmured to Puddles.

But Puddles, curled about Laurie's feet, only snuffled and slept.